HOMETOWN
REUNION

HOMETOWN REUNION

•

Cynthia Scott

AVALON BOOKS
NEW YORK

RoM
S4254 ho

PRINTED IN THE UNITED STATES OF AMERICA
ON ACID-FREE PAPER
BY HADDON CRAFTSMEN, BLOOMSBURG, PENNSYLVANIA

To Mira Son and Avalon Books for allowing me to
bring this story to print.

To Jean Drew for her insightful critiquing.
To Elaine Rierson for her travel agent expertise.

But mostly to my family whose help and inspiration
brought this book to life:
My late father-in-law, Buddy, who inspired Irvin's character.
My husband, Bill (my personal "Geek"), for his knowledge of
the business world.
My sons, Billy and Bobby, for just being themselves.
My brother, Robert, for providing lodging and encouragement
while I did research.
My sister-in-law, Patty, for suggesting Sapulpa as
a backdrop for my story.
And to Sapulpa, Oklahoma, for being the
quaint historic town it is.

Prologue

Fifteen years ago

Ahhhhhh! Barbecued ribs and coleslaw.

Christina Marie Pierce, Miracle High School graduate—with honors—took a deeper breath. The tangy aroma tickled her nose and made her mouth water. Despite the simple wooden tables, the concrete floor and the rough brick walls, the ambiance of Irvin's Bar-B-Q Pit could not be denied.

Mmmmmm. Heaven on earth.

She glanced around the room, etching the image into her memory. Red vinyl tablecloths, cheap plastic vinegar and hot sauce bottles, and a flyer-bedecked front window shouted "hole in the wall" and "dive," but The Pit was *the* teenage hangout in Miracle. Not that Miracle, Oklahoma, a tiny and bedraggled former oil boom town boasted a choice. The Dairy Barn out on the highway tried to cater

1

to the popular crowd, but nothing could beat Irvin's down home, come and stay, eat all night attitude.

Nor his totally scrumptious secret barbecue sauce.

Christi's gaze came full circle to land on the third table from the door, the one by the window, their table—her and her two best friends. They hadn't arrived yet, but Irvin had everything ready for them, right down to the glass mugs bearing their names. She moved to her usual seat, sank into her usual chair and tried to sit still.

Today was the start of something new, something big. Yesterday, she graduated second in her class. Tomorrow, she'd pack up her parents' car and head off for college.

And for a future with Roger.

Mrs. Roger Farley. Christi Farley. Christina Pierce Farley. No matter which version she used, the name sounded perfect. Too bad Roger wanted to wait, wanted to complete their education before they said "I do." Waiting was sensible, but she didn't want to be sensible. She'd been sensible all her life.

She wanted to be spontaneous, to act on her impulses without first weighing the consequences.

Which is why she gave up going to Johns Hopkins and chose to attend college with Roger. Her parents had argued against it, but she could get her nursing training anywhere. If she could do it closer to Roger, all the better. Besides, it was her life, not theirs.

A life with an adventure looming on the horizon.

"Gonna sit there fidgeting or are you going to order?"

Christie snapped out of her reverie to face Glen, The Geek, Stark, also a Miracle High School graduate. Creep. He'd graduated *first* in their class. His dull gray eyes glared at her—as usual—from behind his horn-rimmed glasses. His mud-brown hair coiled on the verge of springing right off his head—as usual. He'd probably come to gloat. As usual. The Geek never struck up a conversation unless he had a point to make. He was the most obnoxious boy in school, and her personal pest.

Unfortunately, he was also Irvin's son. Which meant in addition to seeing The Geek at school, Christi was forced to endure his presence at The Pit, too.

"I'll wait until Amber and Eleanor get here," she said.

"Ah, one redhead, one blond and one brunet. A Triple Threat to common sense everywhere."

"Go away, and let me think."

"About how I graduated top of the class and you didn't?"

Yep, he'd come to gloat. "We were separated by a *tenth* of a point."

"A miss is as good as a mile." He leaned closer, his breath reeking of onions. "Face it. I'm smarter than you, and always will be."

"You're *obnoxious*," she said, waving away the foul fumes. "And always will be."

"I'm not obnoxious." He preened. "I'm perfect."

"You are so *not* perfect," Christi retorted, "that you're not even on the 'perfect' chart."

"MIT disagrees with you."

"MIT?" Ah, the crushing blow. Score a big one for The Geek. More than a little impressed, and more than a lot determined not to show it, Christi forced her voice to stay even. "Massachusetts Institute of Technology accepted *you*?"

"Absolutely." A smug smile curved his lips and his eyes glinted. "This time tomorrow, I'm wiping off the dust of this crummy town and speeding to Boston, never to return."

Dying to find the chink in his armor-plated self-confidence, she handed him a spare napkin. "Better wipe the chocolate milk off your upper lip first."

A muscle twitched in his jaw.

Ah, a direct hit. Score one for her.

"It's a mustache," he said evenly—too evenly.

"It's a complete lack of testosterone," she retorted.

"Like you'd know."

"Oh, grow up," she said, envy nearly choking her words. Imagine MIT, the most prestigious engineering school in the world accepting The Geek. Incredible.

"Tell me something," he said, with that look that said he knew he'd won the point.

"School's out, Glen."

Tell me something was the catch phrase for their mind game of information one-upmanship. She hated it. She always held her own, and often superceded The Geek's mental prowess, but he never gave her a break, never once acknowledged her intelligence, never recognized that, heck, she could go to MIT, too—if she wanted.

She just didn't want to.

"Only for the lazy," he said crisply. "Learning is a continuous experience."

"Go away until you hit puberty. Then stay away."

"I will if you will." Instead of leaving, though, he leaned on the table, palms flat, arms bent at the elbows and peered into her face. "First, I need a bit of trivia."

Christi jerked back, surprised at how appealing his eyes looked when they sparkled. "What?"

"Which college have you picked? Hopefully on the *West* Coast. Or even better, another country."

"I've been accepted to Johns Hopkins," she boasted.

"Unacceptable. Baltimore's *way* too close to Boston."

"I turned them down," she said without thinking. "I'm staying here in Oklahoma and going to school with Roger."

"You're what?" The Geek jerked upright, his face wide open with shock. "You're giving up a prestigious school like Johns Hopkins to stay here in the boondocks? With that idiot? Why?"

"I love him and—"

"No. You can't." He stepped back, a dark frown emphasizing the fledgling mustache. Something flashed in his eyes, something like . . . pain? He blinked and the flash disappeared. "Christi, even *you* are smarter than to settle for Roger the Rat."

"Roger the Rat?" Her temper flared. "Glen Stark, you take that back, or I'll—"

The bell over the door rang, signaling more customers. Christi snapped her head up. Amber Dorsey and Eleanor Host, her best friends since elementary school, entered The Pit. When she turned back to Glen, he'd walked away.

He always disappeared when Amber and Eleanor came around. Christi arched an eyebrow. Threatened, maybe? Hmmm, worth considering. No! She didn't care what Glen Stark thought or felt. Sheesh.

Her friends approached the table. Amber, tall and athletic, flipped her long red ringlets over her shoulder and jerked a thumb toward Glen. "What'd The Geek want?"

"The usual," Christi said. "To tell me I'm stupid."

"Well, he's wrong, as usual." Eleanor, sleek and sophisticated—even at eighteen—tucked a tawny curl behind her ear and smoothed her beige silk dress. "I hope Irvin has one of those big napkins."

"Ready and waiting," Christi said, holding up the cloth lying on the middle chair. "As usual."

She smiled. The daughter of a debutante, Eleanor had

come out the previous month, the only girl in Miracle to do so. Since then her mother insisted she dress only in white, which Eleanor hated, so she rebelled by wearing beige, a color her mother considered tainted.

Eleanor Host, a rebel in pearls and taupe-colored silk.

The two girls took their seats, and the three of them heaved a collective sigh. "After today," Amber said, her golden brown eyes clouding, "nothing will be 'as usual'."

"We have the summer before we have to say good-bye," Eleanor said.

"Um, not really, El," Amber said. "I'm leaving tomorrow."

"What?"

"Me, too," Christi added.

Eleanor's blue eyes dulled. "Both of you? Why? When?"

"Mom's given me the green light," Amber said, flipping her long hair again. "I leave tomorrow to backpack across Europe."

"Amber, that's great!" Christi rose and hugged her friend. Eleanor was the rebel. Amber was the adventurer.

Amber Dorsey, a female Indiana Jones with freckles.

"I can't believe it. We're all realizing our dreams," Christi said. "You're going to Europe, Eleanor's headed for New York and points beyond, and I'm moving to Tahlequah. This is—"

"Tahlequah!" Amber stood, towering over Christi by at least five inches. "Johns Hopkins is in Baltimore, *not* Tahlequah, Oklahoma. Why would you move to Tahlequah?"

"Yes," Eleanor said, rising too. "Explain."

Afraid she was about to be sandwiched, Christi slid between her friends and sat again. "Roger and I are getting married."

"But you're only eighteen!" Amber plopped into her

chair. "This is a mistake, Christi. You're too young. You can't."

"We're not getting married right away."

"Good, then go to Johns Hopkins." Still standing, Eleanor clamped her hands on her hips. "Marry the Rat, uh, Roger after you get your nursing degree."

"I can get my degree anywhere, so why not stay here with Roger?" Christi swallowed and reached for their hands. "I want a career and a family. Don't you?"

"Sure." Amber squeezed her hand first. "But not until I've had some fun. Not until I've seen the world. Right, El?"

Eleanor sat primly and didn't say a word.

"El?" Amber repeated.

"I'm not going anywhere," Eleanor said, her head low and her voice even lower. "And I'm never getting married."

Christi bent to search her friend's face. "Why? What's wrong? What happened?"

"My mother's divorcing my father. He's already moved out. I got a job to help support us."

"Oh, no!" Amber said, shock dominating her face. "What about college? And traveling?"

"I'll be working for a travel agency in Tulsa, so I'll travel. As for school, I'll go at night. After I've saved some money, I'm starting my own business, far away from here."

Christi gave her a one-armed hug. "Eleanor, I'm sorry. What can I do?"

"You can *not* ruin your life with Roger. Use your combination Einstein and Florence Nightingale brain to do something with your life."

"Eleanor, you don't understand," Christi pleaded.

"No, *you* don't understand." Determination blazed in her

bright blue eyes. "Not everyone gets a chance like you have. You can't throw it away on Roger. You just can't."

To Christi's shock, tears plopped onto Eleanor's sculpted cheekbones. She rose, ripped off the napkin and fled The Pit.

"Eleanor, wait!"

Amber rose and spread her hands. "I had no idea. None. El adores her father. This is the worst thing that could happen."

"Go after her," Christi said, her heart breaking. "I'll pay for our order and be over later. We'll get her through this."

Amber nodded and scurried out the door. Christi stared at her empty plate. Today was supposed to be a celebration, a toast to living their dreams, and already one of their trio's dreams had crumbled. She thumped the table. "It's not fair."

"Hey, you break it, you buy it," The Geek said, setting down a tray of ribs, home fries and coleslaw. "What happened to the other two-thirds of the Triple Threat?"

"Go away, Glen, and take the food, too." Christi dropped some money on the table and rose. "Excuse me."

"I always have."

She shook her head, and headed for the door. Today wasn't supposed to go wrong. Nothing was supposed to go wrong. Please let nothing go wrong tomorrow.

At least one thing was certain, one thing had gone right. Starting tomorrow, she'd never have to see, hear, smell or endure Glen, The Geek, Stark again.

Although, in Miracle, nothing was ever truly certain.

Chapter One

W hew! Musty sweat socks and Oklahoma summer.

Christina Pierce Farley took a deeper breath, and the pungent odor invaded her nose and coated her lungs. Despite the black and gold fifteen-year reunion decorations, the DJ blasting rock and roll under the far basketball goal, and the table overflowing with refreshments, the ambiance of the Miracle High School gym could not be denied.

Mmmmmm. Heaven on earth.

Eager to take it all in, she glanced around the room. The reception table beckoned from beneath a banner proclaiming, "Miracle Alumni Do It All." Doubts clenched Christi's stomach and butterflies fluttered wildly. She hadn't done it all. Time to go home.

No.

She'd come back to her hometown to rebuild her life.

Determination squared her shoulders, and after skirting several unfamiliar suit-clad men, she gingerly stepped onto the polished floor. Music vibrated through the wood beneath her feet, reminding her of the thumps of basketball practice and acrobatic cheerleaders at pep rallies. Her stomach unclenched. The cheers of Friday night football games and whispered confidences of teenage girlfriends filled her brain. The butterflies calmed.

Her heels clicked a strong, firm rhythm, until she passed the podium. Memories slowed her quick pace, forcing her to turn and stare. A vision of a young girl clad in a gold graduation robe smiled and waved to the crowd. Christi shook her head. That had been her crowning moment— graduating second in her class. What happened to that confident girl?

Christi searched within, but found only the uncertain woman she'd become.

With a long, deep sigh, she continued to the registration table and pinned on her name tag. Good old Miracle, Oklahoma. She'd spent the happiest years of her life here. Her parents and the small town had loved and nurtured her, giving her a firm foundation for the future. Now, she'd returned, hoping to provide that type of childhood for her sons, Tony and Drew.

"Christi!"

She turned and Amber wrapped around her like a warm scarf in winter. Christi returned the hug with fervor and gazed up at her model-tall friend. "Wow! You look great!"

"So do you, now that you're home where you belong." Smiling, the redhead led Christi to the corner of the crowded gym. "Give it to me straight. Are you all right? I mean, the divorce is final and you're finally free of Roger the Rat?"

"Signed, sealed and delivered."

"Good."

Christi cringed. She'd hated divorcing Roger and separating the boys from their father, but Roger had refused to grow up, to put down roots, to accept his responsibilities as husband and father. Instead, he kept reaching for the brass ring. After ten progressively worse moves in ten years, she'd filed for divorce, packed up the boys and come home to stay.

Forever.

Neither woman spoke. Christi shifted, uneasy in the silence. Finally, Amber gave her an exasperated look. "Well, you gonna show me pictures of your boys or not?"

Christi relaxed and handed Amber her sons' most recent school photos.

She oohed and aahed. "Wow, Tony looks just like you! Same brown hair and eyes. What a cutie. And blond, blue-eyed, Drew. Well, he. . . ."

"It's okay, Amber," Christi said quietly. "There's no denying it. Drew looks like Roger. Thankfully, he's a sweetheart. No clinical evidence of 'Rat' genes."

Amber laughed. "Sounds like you didn't lose your sense of humor." She glanced across the room. "Oh look, here comes El."

Eleanor joined them. If possible, age had improved her classic looks. "Wow," Christi exclaimed, "you look like you just stepped out of *Successful Woman's Weekly*."

Clad in an elegant crepe suit, the tawny-haired woman embraced Christi and smiled. "I am *so* glad you're back."

Warmth spread through Christi until she almost cried. For the last few years, she'd severed ties with family and friends to follow Roger all over the country. Finally, she felt connected again.

Eleanor arched an eyebrow. "Hard to believe it's been fifteen years."

"Yeah," Amber agreed. "Seems like yesterday we were huddling here after graduation, planning our futures."

Christi sighed. "You two certainly attained your goals."

"That's true," Amber said. "I travel the world leading group tours for Miracle Tours, just like I wanted to do."

Eleanor nodded. "And I own Miracle Tours. Amazing. The musings of a couple of teenagers actually came true."

Christi didn't comment. She'd fallen short of her dreams. Graduate school, career, motherhood; she'd wanted it all. Then she'd fallen in love and married Roger. Except for the birth of her sons, her life had gone summarily downhill after that.

She shook off the defeatist thoughts and gazed at her two best friends. "I'm proud of both of you."

"*We're* proud of *you*," Amber said. "It took guts to ditch Roger. How are you holding up?"

"Okay." Christi hugged herself. "The boys had doubts until we moved in with Mama. She decorated their room with superheroes, and had a list of playmates ready and waiting."

"And I have a job for you," Eleanor said. "If you want it."

Christi blinked. "I haven't worked as a travel agent since Drew was born. We moved so much, I—Eleanor, are you sure?"

Amber raised a copper eyebrow. "Is she *sure*? She's yakked about it ever since she heard you were coming home."

"I'm positive," Eleanor insisted. "I need intelligent, competent, friendly people. You are all those things and more."

"Thank you," Christi said softly. "I knew moving home was a good idea."

"Best idea you've had in a long time," Eleanor said.

"Ditto," Amber agreed. "Now, can we forget work and get down to the business of having fun?"

Eleanor's blue eyes sparkled. "Christi does have fifteen years of gossip to catch up on."

"Oh, please, nothing changes in this town," Christi said. *Thank goodness.*

"Don't be too sure," Eleanor said. "Right, Amber?"

"Oh, yeah," Amber drawled. "I think you'll find that not only have things changed, they've done so for the better."

Christi frowned. "What's that's supposed to mean?"

"It means," Amber continued, winking at Eleanor, "have you seen Glen?"

Eleanor winked back. "Gives a whole new meaning to the term 'new and improved'."

"Glen?" Christi's stomach clenched again. "*He's* here?"

Amber nodded. "Oh, yeah."

Christi started to comment, but halted when a deep voice instructed, "Tell me something."

No. Please. Not that. She hadn't played the old "Tell me something I don't know—if you can" game of wits in years. Unless you counted arguing with Roger, which she didn't.

She fumbled, begging her brain to recall some obscure intellectual revelation, but she felt as if she'd been swallowed up by a black hole with nothing but darkness to guide her.

Wait. Black hole. Yes! Squaring her shoulders, she turned. "A black hole occurs when a star collapses, its gravity so dense it pulls—"

Stunned, she stopped in mid-sentence. Gravitational pull was right. Who was the handsome guy with the thick mustache?

"Sorry," he said, his baritone resonant, "no partial credit. I need the complete answer."

Christi's jaw dropped. Coffee-colored wavy hair, simple silver frames over intelligent eyes, firm jaw and broad shoulders spelled only one thing. Impostor. He couldn't be her old adversary. This mouth-watering "hunk of the month" looked nothing like that horn-rimmed, pocket-protected nerd who'd consistently aced her out of first place. Bewildered, she glanced at his name tag for verification. "Glen? Glen Stark?"

"In the flesh." His upper lip twitched, emphasizing the coarse hairs above his mouth. "See? I made it through puberty."

Gives a whole new meaning to the term new and improved.

No kidding. In high school, his mustache had resembled a line of dirt. Now, lush and thick, it rimmed his full lips which currently parted in a dazzling smile.

Wow! Glen the Geek had matured into Glen the Gorgeous. "My goodness, it is you."

"Yes, but this isn't a quiz."

"Good thing, because I didn't study."

"Caught unprepared?" He shook his head. "Tsk. Tsk."

"Why are you here? That is, I heard you were in Boston, or New York. I didn't expect to see you."

"Your fundamental flaw, Christi. You should always expect the unexpected."

"Humph," she said, "and I suppose you're perfect?"

He crossed his arms and smiled smugly, just like the old days. "Good. You finally admit it."

"It was a question, not a statement of fact. Why *are* you here?" she asked again, feeling a smile tug at her lips. Glen still couldn't have a simple conversation with anyone.

Everything, every word became a challenge with him. "School is out. You don't have to check my schedule to make sure we don't have any classes together."

He grinned. "I only did that once."

"Once every year."

"Your memory's faulty."

"No, your ego is—"

"You two have a nice chat," Amber interjected. "El and I are going to check out the other . . . improvements."

"No, wait," Christi pleaded. Rats! The last thing she needed was to battle with The Gorgeous, uh, The Geek. Sheesh! "Um, well, Glen, it's nice seeing you again," she said, ignoring his self-satisfied smirk, "but I'm sure you have other people to harangue."

"I never harangue. I talk."

"You argue."

"Debate would be more concise." His eyes sparkled, as if he enjoyed their exchange.

"If you say so," she said, wishing he'd go away. Marriage to Roger had drained all the fight out of her. That's why she'd moved home, to be with people who accepted her without question.

"If I say so? Is that the best you can do?" He shook his head. "You're losing your touch."

"Give me time," she said. "I just moved back to town."

"Yes, that mind-boggling tidbit roared through Miracle like a springtime tornado, fast and furious."

She arched an eyebrow. "Mind-boggling?"

"As in mentally exciting or overwhelming."

"I know what it means." She was surprised he'd find anything about her mind-boggling, *and* her patience was beginning to wane. "So why are you here? Besides to intimidate me."

"*I* intimidate *you*? That's a revelation."

"As in an enlightening or astonishing disclosure? Now *you're* losing *your* touch. You always claimed you knew everything."

"Everything that's important."

"Oh, please. Puberty changed your body, Glen, but clearly ignored your ego. It's still globally over-inflated."

"You used to say I sported an ego the size of Texas."

"I've expanded my horizons since then."

He shoved his hands in his pockets and studied her. "Really? How?"

Was that concern on his face? No, it couldn't be. "Never mind," she said, realizing she'd almost revealed too much, a definite no-no with Glen—or any man. "You wouldn't understand."

"Christi, wait," he said, tugging on her hand to stop her. "All kidding aside, I'm curious."

"Curious?"

"About you. Why are you back?"

"That kind of curiosity works both ways," she said, still hesitant to give anything away. She'd done that too often with Roger and suffered as a result.

"You mean, you show me yours and I'll show you mine?"

"Excuse me?" For a moment, she just stared. From any other man she'd think he meant . . . no, not The Geek. Confused, she searched his face, but his silvery-blue eyes revealed nothing. "Define your terms."

He laughed, rich and deep. "Let's trade information. Rumor has it you've moved back to Miracle for good."

"True," she said, enjoying the sound of his laughter, and surprised that she did. "Eleanor offered me a job."

"At the agency? I thought you planned to be a nurse like your mom. What happened?"

"Life," she said, blowing out a breath. "I got my degree, but never completed my clinicals to take the state boards."

"Regrets?"

"A few. What about you? What brings you home?"

"Miracle isn't home," he said adamantly. "Not any-more."

"Excuse me, what brings you to Miracle?"

"Visiting my dad."

"Just a stop on the way up the corporate ladder?"

"Something like that," he said. "Actually, I'm on my way to—"

The senior class president approached the microphone and began making announcements.

"Rats," Glen said.

She raised an eyebrow. "What?"

"Time for me to give my speech."

"That's right, you're Miracle's shining star," she said, grinning. "Valedictorian, 'Most Likely to Succeed,' winner of every scholastic award ever conceived. You going to regale us with your achievements?"

"Quite frankly, slipping out the back door crossed my mind."

Her other eyebrow shot up. "Are you kidding?"

"What do you think?" he asked, his eyes revealing noth-ing.

She didn't have a clue, then suddenly remembered his speech at graduation. He'd been very nervous. Could he still feel that way? "Ah, go on, Glen," she said. "Break a leg."

"I'll assume you mean good luck and say thanks," he said, holding out his hand. "Nice talking to you, Christi."

"Yes it was," she said, amazed she meant it, and clasped his fingers in the briefest of handshakes. Warm tingles spread through her palm. "Nice to *match* wits again."

Instead of having them stomped into the ground by Roger.

Glen looked at her strangely, released her and took the stage.

For a moment she did nothing. Her mind buzzed too much, as if awakened from a long sleep and that confused her. Glen's interest confused her. Her palm—that still felt warm from his touch—confused her, too. Before she could make heads or tails of any of it, Glen's voice resonated over the microphone. She glanced up, unable to take her eyes off him. Clad in an obviously expensive navy suit, crisp white shirt and designer frames, he resembled a magazine model.

No one would ever guess he'd been the biggest nerd to almost blow up the high school science lab.

Bewildered by the change in him and by her reaction to him, she strolled to the refreshment table, trying to sort out her thoughts. Glen's baritone spilled out over the gym, friendly, conversational—no signs of nerves—which bewildered her further. Maybe aliens had invaded her brain.

Or maybe she'd been swallowed up by a black hole.

Whatever the reason, Glen had changed and she liked it, and that could only mean trouble.

Glen leaned against the podium and dragged his attention away from Christi. "I'll admit," he said launching into his speech, "that by some *miracle*, I've 'done' a lot." The crowd laughed. "I squeaked by with an engineering degree from Massachusetts Institute of Technology."

"Squeaked?" someone mumbled. "Whatcha do, skip a test and make a 'B'?"

"Something like that," he replied with a grin. "Next I joined a large telecommunications firm and made vice president before age thirty. And last year," he paused again and rolled his eyes, "I purchased my first Mercedes."

Three former lab partners gave him the thumbs up.

"But the road to success is not without roadblocks."

He darted a glance at Christi, who still stood at the refreshment table with her back to him. He'd never, not in a million years, planned to see her again. Why had she come home? Why did he care?

"I married unwisely," he continued, wondering why she wouldn't look at him.

"Been there," someone murmured.

"Then I foolishly divorced."

The basketball captain yelled, "Who got the Mercedes?"

"I did," he said, unable to hide a grin.

"Always knew he was smart," the captain quipped.

Wait, movement from the back of the room. Christi had turned to face him. Good.

"Most recently," he said, "a bureaucratic conglomerate took over my place of employment and I was, yes, you guessed it, I was downsized. Though the term they used was 'right-sized'."

"Who got the Mercedes?" the basketball captain asked again.

"I did," Glen said, laughing out loud. "But what I want to share here tonight is that even roadblocks and dead ends can be viewed as opportunities. Quite frankly, I've always wanted to head up my own company—be my own boss. Now, thanks to USCom, I have the severance to do so."

Applause filled the room and Glen took a deep breath.

Finally, after years of waiting, planning and creating business proposals for this eventuality, he now had the time *and* the money to pursue his dream. He'd sold the house he and his ex-wife had shared, cashed out his stock options and contacted two of his former colleagues with the news. While in transition, he'd visit his father here in Miracle and begin working on some of the legal details of setting up shop in Chicago.

"However," he added, his gaze not only drifting back to Christi, but riveting there, "I have a few other goals, or perhaps dreams is the better word, that I have yet to attain."

"You going to Disney World?" a football star asked.

"Sort of," he said, remembering a particular fantasy that he'd never played out. "I refer to those dreams we all had as kids. Disney World. Walking on the moon. Flying like Superman. . . ."

"Aha!" Christi shouted. "Win one argument with Glen Stark!"

Adrenaline shot through his veins, reviving that old competitive spirit—at least that's what he told himself. "In your dreams!"

The crowd roared with laughter and shouted out comments.

"There they go again."

"Glen and Christi are debating like always."

"Now it feels like Miracle High."

"Hey, Glen," someone shouted, "what are you going to about these dreams? I mean, nobody flies like Superman."

Christi pushed through to the front of the crowd until she stood right in front of him. Tall, dark and handsome, the way the Victorians described women, she could never be classified as beautiful, but the combination of glossy brown hair, luminous brown eyes and scintillating intelligence created a truly stunning woman. And in her simple red dress, she stood out like a beacon he couldn't ignore.

Sweat beaded on his forehead. His pulse picked up, fog smothered his brain and he couldn't concentrate. "What?"

"The question is, Glen," she said, "are any of these un-fulfilled dreams . . . fulfillable?"

He was about to answer, but she smiled—a glinting, glowing, stunning smile—and his mind sped back to high school, to their "tell me something" game. He'd made it his goal to always get the last word, because he'd had a silly teenage crush on Christi and the hormonal surge had driven him crazy. The only way to keep a clear head was to debate, and she was the best debater in school, but she was the cause of his fogged mind. So. . . .

He shook his head, trying to clear his thoughts.

"Glen?" she prompted, smiling wider, "did you hear me?"

"Yes, yes I did," he said, one teenage memory overriding everything else. "There is one dream I could fulfill right now."

"Well, what's stopping you?"

Her expression was classic; the determined jut of the chin, the raised eyebrow and the wide-eyed gaze all meant one thing. She was challenging him.

No way could he refuse a challenge, especially not from Christi, so he stepped off the podium and strode toward her. Later, he'd probably blame his behavior on hormones, ego, or possibly sun spots, but right now Glen acted purely on instinct. He strolled up to Christi, bent her over his arm and planted a loud juicy kiss, smack on her parted red lips.

Chapter Two

Stunned, Christi went limp, and about the time she regained enough control of her muscles to push him away, he stood her upright. Grasping his shoulders—to steady herself—she stared into his eyes. Shock gleamed there, plus . . . enjoyment? Whatever it was quickly disappeared and his expression became unreadable. She opened her mouth to give him a piece of her mind, but her lips were tingling too much to make any sound.

"I did it," he said, his voice a strange, shocked smugness. "I rendered her speechless!"

Applause erupted throughout the crowd and Christi found her voice. "Why, Glen Stark, you—"

"Are perfect. I know." He smirked, gave her a smart salute and made his way out of the gym.

Eleanor and Amber rushed to her side. "Who was that masked man?" Amber quipped.

"I have no idea," Christi mumbled, still suffering from liplock shock.

"Zapped your senses, huh?" Amber said, winking.

"The dip and kiss is so cliché," Eleanor said, shaking her head. "Black and white movie stuff."

"The showoff," Christi said, her senses finally returning. "He stole the show, got the last word. As usual."

"Looked to me like he had something worth showing off," Amber said, her voice dripping with appreciation. "Does he kiss as good as he looks?"

Wow! Double wow! Glen not only looked like a dream, he kissed like one, too. No way would she admit it, though. "His lips were cold."

"Methinks she doth protest too much," Amber said, and laughed. "Until Roger came along, I thought you and Glen—"

"Don't say it," Christi demanded, clamping a hand over her friend's mouth. "You had that bright idea once back in junior high. I gagged then."

"And now?" Amber asked, arching a coppery eyebrow.

"Now, nothing," Christi insisted.

Eleanor shook her head. "Well, hot or cliché, you have to admit he certainly stands out in the crowd."

Christi tried to see the humor in the situation. If her lips would stop tingling, she might even laugh out loud. "He's outstanding in his field," she said wryly, "which is where he should be—out standing in his field."

"Okay, okay," Amber said, "we'll drop it. How about we go to The Pit? Just like the old days. We'll get ribs and coleslaw and those home fries."

"The Pit?" Christi drew back. Glen's father owned Irvin's Bar-B-Q Pit. Would Glen be there? "You two go, I'm going home. Mama's baby-sitting and she's not used to two energetic boys."

"Either we all go, or none of us goes," Amber insisted. "The three . . . what did we call ourselves?"

"Nothing," Eleanor said. "We were too mature for silly nicknames."

"You mean you were too prissy," Amber retorted.

"Stop arguing and let's get a move on," Christi said. "Before you two turn into pumpkins at midnight."

"One for all and all for one!" Amber yelled.

Eleanor walked out the door, rolling her eyes. "That's the 'Three Musketeers'."

Christi laughed outwardly, and silently prayed Glen wouldn't be at The Pit. Masking her emotions had never been one of her strengths and if he saw her flushed face, he'd know she'd enjoyed his kiss. She couldn't give him that satisfaction.

After Roger, she'd vowed never to give a man that advantage again.

Glen stood outside the old high school, staring up at the stars, praying for a cool breeze. Instead, an August blast furnace steamed from the concrete. He shook his head and climbed into his Mercedes. What had possessed him to kiss Christi?

Ego?

Old feelings of inadequacy clouded his mind and he clinched his fists. He'd succeeded, made a name for himself, climbed the corporate ladder two rungs at a time. Why did his hands shake? Why did adrenaline jet through his veins?

Hormones?

The image of Christi filled his brain and his pulse picked up. No, he couldn't be attracted to her. He didn't like her, had never liked her. Sure he'd had a crush on her in high school, but he'd been a teenager, outwardly confident and inwardly clueless. He'd matured in the past fifteen years and knew exactly what he wanted. Argumentative Christi wasn't it.

Sun spots, had to be sun spots. The moon mocked him, but he ignored it.

A movement ahead caught his attention. Three women laughed and talked under the parking lot lights. Eleanor, Christi and Amber, a blond, a brunet and a redhead—still a triple threat to any man's sanity. Well, thank goodness he'd only be in Miracle a few days. He'd visit with his father then head for Chicago to make Stark Communications a reality. Right. Christi wouldn't even figure into the equation.

Eager to prove his point, he quickly started his car and pulled out of the lot.

A few moments later, he pulled up to the back door of The Pit. Situated in the renovated historic center of Miracle, the café occupied an early twentieth–century warehouse, along with several antique shops, boutiques and bookstores. For years, especially since the death of his mother, Glen had begged his father to move to a major city. Irvin Stark created a special sauce that defied description. He could open a chain of barbecue pits and retire a wealthy man.

Except the man claimed he never wanted to leave Miracle.

Bracing himself for an argument, Glen stepped into the immaculate stainless steel kitchen. "Dad, I'm back."

A stocky man with a small mustache and military cut

brown hair poked his head out of the pantry. "You're early."

"You busy?"

"Negative. Too hot for barbecue. All the kids hang out at the Dairy Barn during the summer." Irvin strode to the industrial refrigerator and removed several bags of beef ribs. "You see her tonight?"

Glen blinked. Was his father a mind reader? "See who?"

"The pretty girl who made you sweat in high school."

"I don't know what you're talking about." The image of Christi popped into his mind again, and perspiration beaded on his forehead. Heat of the kitchen. Yeah, that's it. "Why are you cooking ribs if it's too hot for barbecue?"

"The reunion crowd will be here any minute. Yep, you saw her. You're sweating worse than any two pigs."

"It's August and I'm standing over a hot grill. How do you know the reunion crowd's coming here?"

"Don't change the subject. How did she look?"

Glen feigned ignorance. "Who? I saw a lot of women."

His father, the former drill sergeant, stirred a huge pot of sauce and glared at him. "For a smart boy—"

"I'm a grown man, Dad, not a boy."

"—you don't pick up on clues, do you? Was she substandard to your supersonic brain? Is that why you never advanced your position?"

"She's not a military objective, or any objective," Glen said, beginning to get irritated. "She doesn't and didn't exist. Where did you get such an idea?"

"I suffered through your hormonal offensive."

Glen shook his head and moved past him to the swinging door that led to the seating area. "Since you're not busy, I'm going to make some phone calls."

Irvin winked. "So you did see her."

"There is no *her*." He quickly strode to his customary seat in the back booth, flipped open his cell phone and punched in the number for a colleague.

"Neil, how's Atlanta?"

"Glen? Thought you'd fallen off the face of the earth."

Glen relaxed. He and Neil Jackson had worked together at a private telecommunications company on Long Island. When USCom, a huge conglomerate, purchased the small company, Neil left. Glen had stayed only to be downsized half a year later.

"I'm still on the planet, but just barely," he said. "I'm visiting my dad in Oklahoma."

"Hiding from your ex?"

"I don't hide." His marriage had long been over, but he still hated the teasing. "I didn't call to discuss my personal life."

"Wouldn't be much of a conversation, anyway. You live, eat and sleep work."

"And right now I'm investigating a new product opportunity. You interested in a Chief Financial Officer position?"

The line went dead for a moment, then Neil asked, his voice crisp with excitement, "Are you telling me you're setting up your own firm? How? Did USCom give you the rights to SAVEONE?"

"Absolutely. I exercised my golden parachute, negotiated my severance and walked right out with everything on disk. USCom's software division didn't want to waste the man-hours to develop it, but I think they're overestimating the time to market. With the right people, Neil, I can get this out in six months."

"What about start-up capital?"

Glen drew a pen from his breast pocket and started doodling on a paper napkin. "I've roughed out the costs, but I need your expertise."

"Sure, shoot the numbers on over to me. Location?"

"Chicago looks good."

"Who do you know in Chicago?"

"Shana Matthews, VP of operations with SSC Wireless."

"Think you can entice her away?"

"Talked to her last month on another matter. She let it slip they're downsizing."

"I'm sold. E-mail me the business plan."

"Will do. Tonight."

"Great. Talk to you soon."

Glen checked his watch. The Pit would close soon, and he could go home, boot up his laptop and send the information to Neil. The bell over the front door rang, signaling the arrival of customers. He glanced up to see Christi, Eleanor and Amber.

Christi laughed. Glen's pulse sped up.

He drummed his fingers on the wood table and wished he'd gone home instead of coming to The Pit. He didn't want to see Christi, not after making a fool of himself.

Eager to get his attention off of her, he flipped open his cell phone again. Now that Neil was on board, Glen had taken the first step to making Stark Communications a reality. He was impatient to continue and get to Chicago.

Then he could leave the memories of Miracle, and of Christi's sweet lips, far behind.

Christi stepped further inside the restaurant, inhaled the hickory-scented air and said, hopefully, "He isn't open."

Amber pushed past her. "Hey, Irvin, you open or what?"

Irvin instantly appeared and grinned at Christi. "Songbird. Long time no see."

"You haven't called me that in fifteen years."

"Still know all the words to the latest songs?"

"Only children's songs, nowadays."

"Good lookin' children you have, too," he said.

"Oh? When did you see my sons?"

"Your mother showed me pictures. Thought she'd bust a gut bragging on 'em." He turned to Eleanor and Amber, calling them by their teenage nicknames as well. "Princess. Stretch. You want the same table?"

"Please," Christi said.

"Good." He showed them to their usual spot by the front window, crossed to the waitress station and drew out a huge red-checked cloth. With a broad smile, he draped it over Eleanor, tying a knot around her neck. "Can't have your mama chewing me out for ruining your dress, Princess."

Eleanor blushed, but didn't protest. "Thanks, Mr. Stark."

"Irvin," he insisted and winked at Amber. "Sit down, Stretch."

"I *am* sitting down," she protested, then laughed.

Christi laughed, too. Irvin had fondly teased them all. Barely taller than herself, he had constantly pointed out Amber's advanced height, Eleanor's penchant for cleanliness, and her own love of singing. To him nothing had changed, and she thanked goodness for it. "Our usual, please, Mr. Stark."

"Irvin," he said again. "Got the ribs cooking right now."

She raised an eyebrow. "How'd you know we were coming?"

"Where else would you go?"

She laughed again. "True."

Irvin returned to the kitchen and Christi surveyed the long narrow room. After fifteen years, longhorns still decorated red brick walls. Red vinyl lined the seats of the booths and red-checked tablecloths, like Eleanor's "bib," covered the round, wooden tables. Schedules for Miracle's sports teams rimmed the picture window, and an insignia for every business and community organization lined the shelf that ran above the booths. To the right a door led to Irvin's office and a private dining room. A swinging door at the far end led to the kitchen and into the alley beyond.

She continued her survey to the left and her gaze fell on several brightly colored machines. "Video games?"

"He put them in two years ago," Eleanor said. "The antique shop next door folded, so Irvin bought the space."

Christi stared at the half wall separating the café from the game room. "I'm surprised your mother allowed that, Eleanor. I thought she wanted only trendy shops in the historic area."

"How could she object?" Amber asked. "The Rotary Club and the Junior League meet for free in Irvin's back room."

"Mother nearly had a fit." Eleanor grinned. "Especially when I told her I gave Irvin the idea."

"You still don't get along with her, do you?" Christi asked.

Eleanor shook her head. "She puts too much emphasis on appearances. Irvin may not be a southern gentleman, but he's an institution in this town and has served three generations of Miracle teenagers. I couldn't let her or the Pizza Barn take all his customers."

"And the Pizza Barn has video games," Christi said.

"Exactly."

Conversation halted when Irvin returned with drinks, coleslaw and plenty of napkins. "Sure is good to have you home again, Songbird," he said to Christi. "Hope your boys like their bunk beds."

She arched an eyebrow. "You saw their room?"

"Sure." He paused. "I live behind your house, have for over twenty years. Uh, I, ribs will be out in a minute."

Christi gazed at her companions, but their faces wore blank expressions. "What's going on?"

They both shrugged. The swinging kitchen door slapped open, drawing Christi's attention, but only for a moment. Glen sat in the last booth talking on a cell phone, and glanced her way. She bit her lip, then turned back to Eleanor and Amber.

"You two live here. Tell me Glen's not going to be here long," Christi said.

"Okay," Amber said automatically. "Glen's not going to be here long."

Eleanor cut her coleslaw into small pieces, then turned to Christi. "You heard him at the reunion. He's in between jobs—in transition."

Amber leaned forward. "Rumor has it he's looking to start his business in Chicago."

"Rumor?" Christi asked.

"Well," Amber said sheepishly, "Miracle Tours is across the street. I eat here a lot."

"Irvin's not shy," Eleanor added. "He brags on Glen."

Christi sneaked a peek at Glen. He sat alone, just like during high school. Working at The Pit for Irvin had been her first job and while she'd waited tables, Glen had done his homework with his back to the rest of the room. Now he faced them, but focused his attention on his cell phone and something on the table in front of him.

Three days. She'd give him three days before he got tired of small-town life. Type A personalities like Glen had to be doing something all the time. He might be here to visit, but wouldn't do so for long. Her shoulders sagged and she sighed.

"Want to tell us about it?" Amber asked.

"About what?"

"Why you want to know about Glen," Eleanor said.

Several cars of people pulled up outside. "Looks like the rest of the reunion crowd had the same idea we did," Christi said, hoping they'd drop the question. She didn't want to admit, or even think about why she cared about Glen's comings and goings.

Irvin arrived with their ribs. "Here you go, gals. Eat up or no dessert."

Christi glanced around the room, then halted Irvin's retreat. "Where's your staff?"

"Only have two. One home with the flu, the other's got a sick kid."

She frowned. "You can't handle this crowd alone." Several people walked by their table, quickly filling up available booths. "Let me help."

"You bet, Songbird," he said, handing her a tray. "One thing I learned in the Army. Never discourage a volunteer. Get more ribs out of the fridge."

"Shouldn't I take orders instead?"

"Haven't changed the menu in fifteen years." He tapped his head. "Where do you think Glen got his excellent memory?"

Shaking her head, she headed for the kitchen, palmed open the door and froze. Glen stood stirring a pot of sauce, ribs sizzling on the grill to his right. He'd removed his suit coat, rolled up his sleeves and donned an apron. His blue tie peeked out underneath the apron bib, drawing attention to the formality of his attire.

"Thought you were on the phone," she said, pressing her lips together.

His head snapped up. "What are you doing back here?"

"A crowd came in and your father's short-handed. But if you've got it covered. . . ."

Irvin came in, just missing Christi with the door. "What are you standing around for? Dish up the coleslaw. Get more ribs out of the fridge. Line up the platters."

"Dad, Christi's a customer," Glen said, focusing on the pot of sauce he stirred. "You can't put her to work."

"First rule of business, son, never turn down free help." He left the kitchen again.

Glen handed her an apron. "You'll ruin your dress."

"Me? I'm not the one in the Armani suit."

"I have a closet full."

"And I have a lot of dresses," she lied.

He stopped stirring, then looked her down, up and down again. "Not like that one, I'm sure."

The same glint of shock she'd seen after he kissed her flashed through his silvery-blue eyes. She blinked. He'd never approved of anything of hers—not that she cared. She clamped one hand on her hip. "What's wrong with this dress?"

"Nothing."

"It was a Christmas present from my mother."

"That explains the color."

"You don't like red?"

"It's fine."

"Just fine? Come on, Glen, for once say what you feel, not what you think."

He turned back to the grill and muttered, "If you're going to work, put on the apron and get to it."

She couldn't understand him. Usually, he got right in her

face, daring her to find a hole in his logic. Why wouldn't he look at her? Was it possible the kiss affected him, too?

Ah, maybe she had an advantage. Hmmmm. Overcome by the urge to challenge him and win, she straightened and gave him a smart salute. "Sir, yes, sir."

"Finally accepted the fact that I know what I'm talking about?"

She looped an apron over her head and rolled her eyes. "Oh, please. I've forgotten more than you'll ever *think* about knowing."

"Is that so? Then tell me something."

"Okay. Your kiss doesn't count."

The tongs he'd been holding clattered to the floor. "Excuse me?"

"You're excused. I'm glad you accept your defeat."

"That's not what I meant and you know it."

"Oh?"

"Absolutely. After all," he added dryly, "I got the last word."

"Not to my way of thinking."

"Which is illogical as always."

"Nope." She clucked her tongue. "Merriam Webster's Collegiate Dictionary—the Tenth Edition—defines 'last word' as the final remark in a *verbal* exchange, meaning words. Kisses aren't words."

"What do you do, carry a dictionary around with you?"

"I looked it up long ago and expressions of a physical nature, such as kissing, are not verbal. So, I win."

"Not quite. You said final remark in a verbal exchange, right?"

"Yes," she said, wary. "So?"

"So my kiss represented the final *remark*," he said, that

self-satisfied smirk returning. "And that's all that's required. So I win. Perfectly logical."

"Except I find nothing logical about *you* kissing *me*."

Irvin poked his head in. "Will you two stand down your fighters and start slinging some hash?"

"Yes, sir." Glen straightened. "Coming right up."

Christi gave thanks for the interruption then stopped short and heat flushed her cheeks. Had Irvin heard their discussion? Of course he had—just like every other time she and Glen worked in the kitchen together. They'd never gone more than three minutes without arguing. Rats! This was not what she had in mind when she moved back to Miracle. Not at all.

She let out a breath and picked up a tray while Glen heaped ribs onto a platter. When she started toward the door, something caught, jerked and spun her right into Glen.

"Careful." His voice cracked. "You almost knocked me into the grill."

"Sorry." She tried to edge away and nearly bumped him again.

"Wait, your string's hung up." He freed her from the drawer. "Try tying them next time."

"Important safety tip. Thanks." Heat flushed her cheeks again, but she blamed it on working in a hot kitchen in August, and moved to the island work counter to put down the tray.

"What are you doing?"

"Going to tie my apron."

"Don't move, or you'll spill all three of those dinners. I don't feel like mopping up barbecue sauce. Do you?"

"Then how do you suggest I tie the apron?"

"I *suggest* you stand still and let me do it."

As he moved up behind her, she clamped her eyes shut and tried to focus on keeping the tray steady. Not on how nice he smelled, or how much she enjoyed their verbal sparring. When his arms came around her to tie the strings in front, her knees nearly buckled. Aliens *had* invaded her body. No way on earth would she have believed she'd ever be attracted to Glen Stark.

"The strings were too long to tie in back," he said as though he felt the need to explain.

"Of course." If only she had an explanation for this weird attraction, but she didn't have a clue. "All done?"

"Absolutely."

"Thank you," she said, and rushed into the seating area.

"You okay, Songbird?" Irvin asked.

"I forgot how hot it got back there."

"Hot, huh? Why don't you two don't just face facts? You already square off like an old married couple, so go ahead and make it legal. You know you're perfect for each other."

She forced herself to laugh—to maintain her sanity. "Sarge, you're out of your mind."

"Maybe." He looked her over with the same silvery-blue eyes Glen had. "But I recognize sparks when I see them flying."

"I have no idea know what you're talking about. Now if you'll excuse me, I need to serve these ribs."

She scooted past him, but not before she caught the glint of satisfaction in his gaze. She groaned inwardly. Why had Glen kissed her? Why was Irvin talking like her future father-in-law? There was nothing between her and Glen, and there couldn't be.

Determined to nip the whole thing in the bud, she served a table of former classmates and made a vow. She'd avoid Glen during his short stay. That way, everyone, especially the local gossips would see tonight had been another of her and Glen's games. They'd realize she had no interest in the man. None.

As soon as she caught her breath—and her lips stopped tingling—she'd try and convince herself of that, too.

Chapter Three

No matter how hard he tried—and he put in a lot of effort—Glen couldn't get Christi out of his mind. Her smile, her scent, the lilt of her voice lingered long after The Pit closed, and invaded his dreams, too. When he woke and stumbled into the kitchen for coffee, she still hovered in his brain. Of course, the fact that he had a perfect view of her backyard, where, in worn shorts and a faded Baltimore Orioles T-shirt, she knelt near her mother's prize flower bed and pulled weeds, might have something to do with it.

"Quite a night," Irvin said suddenly.

Startled, Glen almost dropped his mug, and, glad for the distraction from Christi, turned to his father. "Always amazes me how efficiently you handle a crowd."

"Army training."

Glen picked up a napkin and wiped the coffee that had splashed over. "I meant it as a compliment, Dad."

"No, you meant it as the beginning of the 'Why don't you sell franchises?' speech."

"Franchises are a gold mine," Glen said, his gaze never leaving the sight of Christi tugging at errant Bermuda grass.

"You're the entrepreneur in the family." Irvin poured himself a cup of coffee. "Not me."

He sat at the table, blocking Glen's view. Glen automatically leaned back to keep Christi in sight.

Irvin glanced over his shoulder. "Storm coming or something? We could use some rain."

"Storm? What storm?"

"The storm going on in your brain, Son. What's eating you—besides my lack of ambition?"

More like his heart, Glen thought, but he wasn't going to admit that. "I never said you lacked ambition."

"You thought it. Ever since those prestigious colleges fought over you, you've looked at your old man as a failure."

Glen let out a long breath. "Owning the local teenage hangout has its merits."

"I'll tell you what has merit. Serving your country. Being a good citizen. Raising children with good, solid values."

Glen gripped his new fifteen-year reunion commemorative Miracle High School mug. "You know my ex-wife never wanted children."

"But you did. Why did you marry her?"

"Because she was—"

"Self-serving, conniving, manipulative—"

"Dad!"

"You know I'm right. She never wanted what you wanted."

"You're wrong. She—"

Two young boys joined Christi in the yard. The tallest, dark-haired like his mother, rolled a soccer ball between his feet. The other, fair and wearing glasses, seemed oblivious to everything but the small airplane he carried. Christi raised up, gave both boys a hug, and nodded toward the house.

Hollowness echoed within Glen. "My ex showed me the light. I don't have the temperament to be a father. I'm too focused on my career," he said, the words tasting bitter on his tongue. "Children need parents who'll be there for them."

"Like Christi is for her sons, you mean."

"Christi has nothing to do with it."

He indicated the view through the patio door. "She's a good mama. That's for sure. Look at her. You can see the love in her eyes from here."

Glen feigned ignorance. "Where?"

"You never were a good liar, son. *That* you got from me."

"What's your point?"

"You're the last of the Starks. You don't get married and have babies, the line will die out."

"It would be a crime for me to have children," Glen said, hating to admit it. "I don't relate to kids. Never have. Even when I was one."

"You think people are born good parents? It's on-the-job training. Tough, too." He shuddered. "I'd rather march twenty miles every day with a full pack."

"Thanks a lot."

"Ah, stop acting like I hurt your feelings," Irvin said and refilled his coffee cup. "You know I'm proud of you. I'm just saying if an old soldier like me can be a dad, anybody can. But if you had someone who was already an expert to help. . . ."

Glen shook his head. "You're barking up the wrong tree, Dad. Christi and I don't even like each other." Even if he did choose to marry again—and raise a family—he wouldn't do it with a woman from Small Town USA. "My opportunities for success lie in big cities; New York, LA, Chicago."

"Bull."

Glen's temper rose. So did he. "What does that mean?"

"Your idea of success is wrong. That's what."

"Is this the 'relax and enjoy life' speech?" Glen asked through clenched teeth.

"Don't be insubordinate," Irvin snapped, then let out a long breath. "Sorry. Old habits die hard. Since your mother died. . . ."

Glen cringed. His mother had died when he was ten. Grief-stricken, Irvin had fallen back on his military training to guide him as a single parent. He gave the orders. Glen followed them, and insubordination was not tolerated. That method got them through the tough times, but also kept them from being close.

Something Glen had always regretted.

He stared now at his slightly shorter, but always more determined father, when a scream erupted from Christi's backyard. Without thinking he bolted out the back door.

And caught a face full of cold water.

"Uh-oh," a small voice said.

"What in the world?" Water dripped off Glen's nose, trickled down his shirt and onto his shorts. Small rivers ran down his legs into his socks, making mush out of his running shoes. Through his splattered glasses, he made out Christi's figure clamping her hands on her hips.

"Uh-oh is right, young man," she said. "See what happens when you horse around?"

The blond boy jumped out from behind a large redbud tree. "Tony's going to get it. Tony's going to get it."

"Drew, stop teasing your brother," Christi admonished. "Tony, apologize."

"Gee, Mom, it was an accident," Tony said. "I was filling the pool and Drew distracted me. . . ."

Glen removed a damp handkerchief from his pocket and wiped his glasses.

Christi glanced at him, then seemed to chew her lip. "At which time you sprayed me," she said, indicating her wet legs.

"Yeah and you screamed," Tony said.

"That water's cold. In this heat, it's a shock."

Glen satisfactorily dried his glasses and really looked at her. She looked sixteen again: young, fresh, confident, and prettier than ever. He shook his head. The sweltering August heat had given him sunstroke.

"Really, Mom," Tony continued, "your scream scared me. I jerked the hose—"

Scared him, too. *That's* why his mind was fogged. Yes, that made sense.

"—and accidentally drenched our neighbor," Christi finished for him.

"Yeah."

"Hand me the hose, then please get Mr. Stark a towel."

Tony complied and Glen's gaze riveted to the woman who'd overtaken his mind. Her umber-colored hair, long and silky in high school, now barely brushed her nape. Her mocha brown eyes gleamed with parental authority and her full lips pressed together in concern. Still holding the garden hose, she patted her bare foot while the boys completed their tasks.

She embodied the small-town mom—just the type of woman Glen wanted to avoid.

Right. Avoid.

Tony returned with a fluffy beach towel embroidered with the words "Ocean City, Maryland." Christi laid a hand on her son's shoulder. "Now apologize."

Tony looked up at him and the resemblance to Christi struck Glen like a kick to the gut. What would it be like to gaze into his mirror image every day? Forget it. He had a business to get off the ground, a new product to market.

"I'm sorry, Mr. Stark."

The genuine sorrow in Tony's dark eyes struck a chord in Glen, a memory of how awkward he'd felt at age ten and he shrugged. "I don't usually take a bath until Saturday night, but it does feel cooler. No harm done."

Drew popped up. "Mr. Stark? Is your name Glen?"

He nodded.

"You don't look like a geek. Mom told us about how you two argued and how she always won because she was smarter—"

"Drew, that's enough!"

Glen's noticed Christi's cheeks flush slightly and smiled to himself. "Your mom told you wrong," he said, crossing his arms over his chest. "I always won, because *I'm* infinitely smarter."

Icy water bombarded his face and he sputtered. "What in the world?"

"Tsk. Tsk. Glen. Don't you know you should always expect the unexpected?"

Memo. Never tease Christi when she's holding a water hose.

Irvin roared with laughter from the back porch. "Good thing you have that towel," he said and laughed again.

"Mom!" Tony took the hose and dropped it into the pool. "I can't believe you did that."

Glen attempted to dry himself off—again.

"Go get your swimsuits on," she said to the boys.

Glen glared at her, willing her to apologize. Instead, her shoulders shook and she erupted with laughter. "I always said you were all wet."

"Ha-ha."

"All those years I groped for the right words to bring you down a peg. I should have turned the garden hose on you." Clutching her stomach, she bent over and collapsed to the grass. "If you could only see how you look."

"Like a drowned rat," Irvin said from behind them.

Glen shook his head, flinging droplets everywhere. His father wasn't the only one watching. Half the neighbors grinned and pointed. "No privacy," he muttered.

Nothing had changed. Four-foot chain-link fences separated the lots, affording a view to infinity. From where he stood, he could see three houses in each direction, plus several on Christi's side of the street. Everyone saw, heard and snooped into everyone else's business.

Anxious to get out of the spotlight, he handed her the Ocean City beach towel and backed up.

Christi calmed her giggles and waved to several people. "I'm sorry I startled you, Glen, and thanks for not being hard on Tony."

"No problem." He turned and headed for his house.

Irvin lounged at the back door, grinning ear to ear. "All washed up, are you?"

"Everyone's a comedian today."

"Just don't drip all over the carpet."

Glen strode to his room and closed the drapes so he couldn't see Christi anymore. He had no business fantasizing about her. She had attained an earthy quality—like a tree putting down roots. He didn't want roots. He wanted to be free to move around, to take whatever opportunity came up. Until he left town he'd stay away from the back windows.

Irvin walked into the room and leaned against the door-jamb. "How long until you get Stark Communications up and running?"

Glen grabbed a towel and dried his hair. "If I'm lucky, a few months, but it could take longer."

"You gonna buy or rent a house for yourself?"

"Rent at first, then buy. In my tax bracket, I need the deduction." He grinned, hoping his father caught the joke. Since he was technically unemployed, he didn't have a tax bracket. "But a condo, not a house."

Irvin frowned. "I don't claim to know much about tele-communications, but I've run a business for a lot of years. Seems to me you need to save money where you can."

"Absolutely. What's up, Dad?"

"Why not set up temporary headquarters here? You got a free bunk and plenty to eat. Your only expenses will be long distance calls and faxes and legal mumbo jumbo. You could pocket the cash you'd throw away on one of those high-priced city apartments, and put it where it belongs. In Stark Communications."

First Glen dropped the towel, then his jaw followed suit. "Stay here?" He glanced around his minuscule room. Patriotic-themed curtains covered the narrow window. High school awards, banners and newspaper clippings blanketed the royal blue walls, and red carpet covered the floor. A squeaky bed angled across the corner. A student desk and shelves sat near the door. He felt like he was ten again. He couldn't work from this room.

Behind him, sounds of splashing and squealing filled the silence. Christi's sons obviously enjoyed the water. No, he couldn't stay.

He reached down and picked up the towel. "No."

"Why not?"

"Because we'd drive each other crazy."

"If you work as hard at getting your business up and running as you studied in high school, I'll never see you. Not to mention that when school starts, the joint'll start jumping again and I'll be at The Pit most of the time. Besides, you could visit with some of your old friends before you run off again."

"I'm not running off, Dad," Glen said, examining his father's drawn features again. "I'm working on my career."

"Right. Forget it." In rigid military style, he squared his shoulders and marched away.

Glen shook his head. What a crazy idea. No way would he stay in Miracle a moment longer than necessary. Gossip and the small town's snail pace would drive him crazy.

Wait a minute. What had Dad said, The Pit would start jumping after school started? Did that mean nights like the previous one? Of course Irvin had been short-handed, but this morning he'd slept past nine. For all of Glen's life, reveille had blown at six in the morning.

The truth hit him like a blow.

Irvin enjoyed good health and had a lot of years left, but was definitely showing signs of aging. The moment Stark Communications incorporated, Glen would be knee-deep in work and the opportunity for a long visit with his father would be practically nonexistent.

"Dad?"

"Yeah?"

Glen found him in the kitchen, leaning against the avocado green laminate counter. Dark circles shadowed Irvin's eyes and lines etched his mouth. He looked exhausted.

"I'll need to put in a second phone line," Glen said quietly. "Maybe rearrange the furniture. That okay with you?"

"You foot the bill, son, and you can build the Taj Mahal for all I care."

"Then I accept your offer."

To his surprise, Irvin hugged him. "Great. I always knew you were smart."

Glen smiled, and made the mistake of glancing out the patio door. Through the gaps in the mimosa tree and his mother's lilac bush, he could see Christi. Laughing and squealing, she launched herself into her sons' wading pool, splashing out half the water and drenching all three of them.

He desperately wanted to join them, to play and splash, and he didn't even like water.

I must be losing my mind to stay here.

"Yeah, I'm smart," he said, forcing himself to ignore the sounds of glee—and his wish to join them. "Smart enough to get this company off the ground before the end of the year."

"Then you'll be here for Christmas?"

"I doubt it. But we can trick-or-treat together."

"Very funny."

Irvin's smile drooped a bit, but Glen had to guard himself: from his father's "stay at home" attitude, from the laidback pace of the town, and from Christi. With only a darting glance to her, he checked the calendar. Late August. With luck, he'd be out of here by the first of October.

Irvin walked over to the freezer and drew out two frozen

chunks of meat. "Steak for dinner tonight," he said. "To celebrate."

Glen studied his father's drawn features again. Maybe he shouldn't be in too big a hurry to get away. No, he'd better stay until the end of October. But the instant he insured his father would make it, he'd wash off the dust of this tiny town and head back to the real world.

Chapter Four

"Glen's been here over a week," Christi mused aloud while sipping her coffee. "I can't believe it."

"Irvin talked him into a longer visit," her mother said.

Christi gazed across the kitchen table at Lillian Pierce. Short gray hair framed her face, emphasizing the sparkle in her brown eyes, and her skin glowed with good health. In comparison, Christi felt old. Struggling with Roger's schedule and demands had sapped her energy. "How do you know that?"

"Uh," Lillian's cheeks pinked up, "Irvin told me."

Christi arched an eyebrow. "Mama, are you blushing?"

"I never blush," Lillian said, clearing her throat. "Irvin is my neighbor and we talk. That's all."

"Exactly what he said," Christi said, curiosity nearly choking her words. "He complimented me on the boys' bunk beds."

"Really?" Again, her mother blushed. "Well, he raised a son, knew what they liked. I, um, asked his advice."

Wait a minute. Could her mother be interested in Glen's father? No way. "Mama, what—" Christi began, but Tony appeared, preventing further "grown-up" talk.

Giving him a big smile, she reached out and ruffled his dark hair. "Good morning, Dude."

He grinned—sort of. "Hey, Dudette."

"Ready for school?"

"School is for dweebs."

Christi understood his reaction. Tony had trouble in every subject, mainly because Roger had moved them so often. Hopefully the stability of Miracle would get him back on track.

"Hey, Mom!" Drew jumped out from his room into the hall, his shirt halfway tucked into his shorts. "Is it time for school, yet? Shouldn't you go to work? Can we walk to school?"

Tony moaned. "See what I mean? School is for dweebs."

"Don't call him names, Tony," Christi said gently. "Drew's excited."

"Yeah." Tony yawned, and added sarcastically, "Me, too."

"Come on Drew, eat your breakfast," Christi said. "Yes, I should go to work, and yes, you may walk to school— with Tony."

Tony groaned. "Ah, Mom."

"Can I have my friend come over and play today?" Drew asked.

"That's up to Grandma," Christi said.

Lillian didn't miss a beat. "That sweet little Danny across the street? Sure. Tony, you want a buddy to come over, too?"

He brightened, but tried not to show it. "I guess."

Lillian nodded. "Great. We'll bake cookies."

Drew hurried over and gave her a swift hug. "All right, Grandma! I love you."

"Yeah, me, too," Tony said.

Christi fought back tears. In less than a month, *both* boys had made friends. Plus, her mother seemed to thrive on having a crowd of children around. Twice this week, Christi had come home to a yard full of eight- and ten-year-old boys.

Thank goodness for small towns and family.

She kissed her mom's cheek, then hugged and kissed each son. "You be good, both of you. I love you."

"I love you, too, Mom," Drew said, "and don't worry. We'll be so good for Grandma you'll think aliens invaded our bodies!"

She laughed. "I'll believe that when I see it. Bye now."

On the way to work, she let the tears flow. If only Tony would tell her what bothered him, but her ex-husband had taught him to "Be a man and take life's punches without tears."

Drew hadn't listened, but Tony had taken it all to heart.

Turning off Main Street onto Route 66 and into the Miracle Tours parking lot, she scolded herself. Crying wouldn't help anything. She needed to have faith that in time Tony would adjust and be his happy, smiling self again. With renewed hope, she blew her nose and stepped into the office.

Miracle Tours, across from The Pit, occupied a portion of the bottom floor of an early twentieth–century warehouse and was decorated with Victorian antiques of honeyed oak. Warm greens and cool blues dominated the upholstery, the Persian rug and the brocade wall paper. Christi stopped in the foyer and checked her reflection in the antique gilt mirror.

Eleanor, perfectly dressed as usual, cocked an eyebrow and approached. "Problems?"

"Tony's having a hard time settling in."

"And the struggle is difficult to watch."

"Yes," she said, biting her lip to stem more tears. "Very hard. Thanks for understanding."

"Good morning, Christi." Amber joined them, looking stunning in a jade silk pantsuit. "Hey, you okay?"

"I will be," Christi said, "eventually."

"We'll get you through it," Eleanor said.

"Definitely," Amber agreed. "We're here for you."

"You two are the best," Christi said, beginning to believe her life might straighten out after all. "I'm glad I came home."

"So am I. You're doing a great job," Eleanor said, patting her shoulder. "Speaking of which, what do you say we get to work and see how many round-the-world tickets we can sell today."

"Yeah!" Amber said and hurried to her seat.

Braced by her friends' comforting words, Christi strolled to her desk, donned her headset and positioned her fingers above the keyboard, ready to face the next challenge.

Unfortunately, her next challenge waltzed in looking handsome, appealing and completely irresistible. Glen.

She took a deep breath and muttered, "Give me strength," before saying aloud, "May I help you?"

"Yeah," he said, frowning, "I need to make a reservation."

Her heart thumped an irregular beat. Sure, Glen attracted her, but she could ignore it, if she kept the conversation light—and adversarial—like the old days.

Somewhat hopefully, she asked, "Running away from home?"

"Don't you wish. It's business."

"Why didn't you call?" *And save me from having to stare into those compelling intelligent eyes.* "I could have brought the tickets home and 'airmailed' them over the back fence."

"No thanks," he said, a grin curving his lips. "I already suffered your poor aim when you sprayed me with the water hose."

"Poor aim? Hah! I could always tie a rock to them and chuck it at your head. No way I'd miss something that large."

"I doubt you could hit the broad side of a barn, and I certainly don't see any baseball scouts lining up at your door."

"Because you never look beyond your own nose."

"Quite frankly, I'm always looking beyond my nose," he said, narrowing his eyes. "It's a big world out there, Christi."

Another jet-setter. Roger used to spout the same words. *It's a big world out there, Christi, let's explore it.* Then he'd take a job in a new city, leaving her to pack and follow. Well, she was sick of exploring, of packing, and of following.

"I've seen enough of the world," she said, fighting to keep the edge from her voice. "I'm fine right where I am."

"Oh?" His expression softened. "How much is enough?"

Unsure if he was baiting her, she hesitated. Oh, why not tell the truth? "Ten different cities in ten years."

He arched an eyebrow. "You're kidding."

"No way. If I never move again, it will be too soon. I've

considered nailing my feet to the floor, but haven't figured out how to drive with two-by-fours on my shoes."

"So," he said, chuckling lightly, "you're here for good."

"And you're on your way out."

"Absolutely."

Good. Thankful that was out in the open, she turned back to business. "So, where to?"

"Round-trip to Chicago." He eyed her, as though she'd said something he didn't understand. "Two days. Plus car and hotel."

Rats, only two days. That would barely give her time to breathe, much less forget how much she'd enjoyed his kiss, being near him. Still, her fingers flew over the keyboard. "Rumor has it you're setting up your business there," she said, trying to concentrate on the numbers on the screen.

"I lived there before New York," he said. "Liked it. Still have contacts there."

"I liked it, too, except for the snow."

"Chicago was one of the ten?"

"We lived there eight months—September to April." A shiver ran down her spine. "During a huge snow storm, both boys came down with the chicken pox. We were stuck inside for over a week. The pharmacy and the pizza place down the block delivered. If it hadn't been for them. . . ." She shuddered. "Hotel preference?"

"Something downtown."

She typed in a request and pointed at the monitor. Glen leaned in close and his outdoorsy scent washed over her. Wow! "This hotel offers an airport shuttle and is convenient to public transportation," she said, trying to think of a way to stop breathing in his tangy aroma and still live, "so you won't need a car. Unless, of course, you need to go out of the city."

She glanced up at him and her lungs stopped inhaling on their own. He was so close, so kissable.

"No," he said, staring at her mouth. "No."

"No?"

"I can't," he insisted and cleared his throat. "I mean I don't need to leave the city. A shuttle will make life easier."

Easier? Nothing with Glen had ever been easy. "Are you planning on locating your office downtown?"

"Yes. Why?"

"My next-door neighbor in Chicago was married to a commercial real estate agent. He handled a lot of downtown office space. I could give you his name."

Glen scowled and Christi chided herself for speaking up. Every time she'd offered to help Roger, he'd dismissed her ideas as ludicrous. Why set herself up for that with Glen?

"Never mind," she said. "You probably have an agent looking already. That's why you're going on this trip."

"I do, but no one I know personally." He rubbed his jaw and eyed her, again as if she'd said something he didn't quite understand. "Why would you want to help me?"

To get you away from me. You're too unsettling for me.

"I'd like to help *him.*" Which was partly true. "He and his wife were really good to the boys and me that winter."

Glen seemed to think about that for a moment, then nodded. "In that case, thanks. I'd appreciate his name."

She took one of her new business cards and wrote the name on the back. "Here you are."

"Thank you. I'll call this guy right away."

She smiled, amazed how good she felt that Glen took her suggestion. "Tell him I said hello, will you, please?"

"Will do."

Curious when he intended to leave Miracle for good, she said, "Tell me something."

"A black hole results from a star going supernova—"

She groaned, realizing she'd used the buzz word for their game of wits. "No, I mean, educate me about something."

"Absolutely," he said, his eyes flashing with interest. "Red is my absolute favorite color."

"What?" Christi blinked, unsure she'd heard him right. "What did you say?"

"I said—" His pager vibrated, and he drew it from his pocket. "Excuse me, I've got to leave," he said after looking at the readout. "I'll stop by later and pick up the tickets."

"Right," Christi said, still bewildered. "See you then."

Unable to help herself, she stared at his retreating form. Red was Glen's favorite color? Did that mean he liked her red dress, or that he didn't like her because she wore red? Confused, she took a long drink from her water bottle.

Eleanor strolled over. "Makes your mouth go dry, huh?"

"The Geek?" Christi said, forcing nonchalance into her voice. "Are you out of your mind?"

"Geek, schmeek. He has money, a great body and a brilliant mind. Sounds like a prime catch to me."

Christi's jaw tightened, and she scolded herself. She *wasn't* jealous. "He's moving to Chicago. "You'd never see him."

Eleanor winked. "Who said I was talking about me?"

"You're the one drooling."

"And you don't find him . . . drool-worthy?"

Christi found him very drool-worthy, but she'd felt the same about Roger and that had been a disaster. "He's improved since high school. A little."

"I'd forgotten how stubborn you are, Christi."

"Being stubborn is the only way I've survived."

Eleanor opened her mouth to speak, then sighed and walked away. Christi took another long drink of water and returned to her computer. Glen Stark didn't affect her. Not one bit.

Yeah, and pigs fly.

Christi struggled to not ponder Glen's curious *red is my favorite color* statement. He was a duplicate of Roger, more polished, but still a jet-setting, career-minded man who would only break her heart, and she couldn't let him affect her.

Yet, she couldn't get him out of her mind.

When he returned from Chicago, she struggled harder, because she saw him everywhere. When she went shopping, she nearly plowed into him in the frozen food aisle of Miracle Foods. When she needed stamps, she stood behind him—awash in his outdoorsy scent—at the Miracle post office. At Miracle Cleaners, she brushed his shoulder as he came out and she went in.

It took a miracle to keep from reaching out to him, to ask exactly what the *red is my favorite color* statement had meant.

Tonight, though, she'd be safe. Tonight, she and the boys were going to sign up for Cub Scouts. Glen had no reason to be within a hundred yards of that place.

Unfortunately, when she stepped over the threshold of the elementary school cafeteria, her security fled.

Behind the Cub Scout registration table sat Glen Stark.

"What's the matter, Mom?" Tony asked, clenching her hand.

"Nothing," she hedged. How could she have forgotten?

Irvin was Scout Master. He'd obviously dragged Glen along to help register the newcomers.

"Once more into the breach," she said under her breath. "Let's go, Tony," she said aloud and added, "Come on, Drew."

As always, Drew lagged behind, pausing to examine something or other. If it had buttons, dials or switches, Drew had to touch it, hence his nickname, "The Engineer." Except sometimes he "touched" things too well and they came apart.

Drew joined them as Christi entered the large room, and Irvin rushed over to greet her. "Songbird!"

"Hi, Mr. Stark."

Christi smiled and quickly introduced her sons—though the three of them had been talking over the back fence for days. Tony quietly shook Irvin's hand, while Drew raced to join two boys he recognized from his third-grade class.

Irvin indicated the registration table. "Go sign up, Tony."

Tony didn't move. Christi squeezed his hand. She knew, unlike Drew, he didn't recognize anyone. In all their moves, Cub Scouts had always welcomed her boys with open arms, but Tony needed a buddy or he wouldn't join in. Together they slowly crossed the beige tile floor to where Glen sat handing out forms.

"I see your Dad put you to work again," she said, trying to keep the conversation neutral.

"I *volunteered*," he said, his voice tight, and his eyes held none of the interest she'd seen at the travel agency. Had she imagined it? "Tony, you joining up?"

"Yes, sir," Tony said quietly.

"Show me your hands."

Tony hesitated, then held out his hands, palms up.

Glen inspected them and winked. "Good. No water hose."

To Christi's delight, Tony laughed and said, "I must have left it in my other pants."

Glen laughed, too, and suddenly seemed to relax. "Thank goodness. Hey, have you grown in the last week?"

"I'm five feet tall, today," Tony declared, stretching to his full height. "Seven more inches and I'll be as tall as Mom."

"Even taller, then you can look down on her." He grinned at Christi and added, "Huge benchmark in a boy's life to be taller than his mom."

"Yeah!" Tony agreed, then a neighbor boy came running up and whisked him away.

Surprised by Glen's understanding attitude, Christi bent to fill out the forms. "I thought *your* benchmark was to be taller than me."

"It was," he said, smiling like he had a secret. "Then."

"Took you till ninth grade to do it, though."

"Yeah, but I made it."

Oh, yeah, he made it all right. Christi glanced up from the papers and examined his face, his eyes and his delicious mustached mouth. He made her want to fall in love all over again—something she'd vowed never to do.

"Tony will make it before then," she said, sticking to a safe subject.

"True. He seems like a great kid."

"He is. They both are," she said, love for her sons softening her voice. "I'm a lucky mom."

"Yes, you are." His voice took on a note of wistfulness and the interest she'd seen sparkled in his eyes again—she thought. "Well, lucky mom," he added, his voice even again, "you're signed up and ready to rock and roll."

"Thank you." She smiled at him, intrigued, until he handed her the forms and his fingers brushed hers.

Be tough. Don't let him get under your skin.

"Thought you'd be on your way out of town by now," she said a little too crisply.

"So did I," he answered, just as crisply.

"What's keeping you?"

"A few things. Visiting my dad, for one."

"And the others?"

"Well," he said, his gaze dropping to her mouth, "I'm not at liberty to say."

"Oh, well, um. . . ." She lost herself in his gaze, her memory fleeing back to the kiss and the closeness in The Pit's kitchen. "Well, Irvin seems to be happy to have you around."

"And you aren't?"

"What?" Why did he care and why was he so cryptic? In the old days when he had an opinion, he spat it out. Why not now?

"Simple question," he said.

"Nothing about you is simple. Never has been."

Irvin stepped between them. "If you two are through squabbling, I'll start the meeting."

"Sorry." Christi blushed and headed for the chairs. Irvin started talking, but she had a hard time listening. Instead her mind spun with questions. What could induce Glen to linger in Miracle? He'd never like the small town, claimed it limited him.

Then again, why did she care? Maybe she should stop searching for a hidden agenda and take Glen at his word. Maybe he simply wanted to visit his father. Her gaze slid over to where he stood in the corner, his cell phone to his ear, his back to the room. Yes, that had to be it.

Satisfied, she turned her attention to the meeting and hoped her control would hold out longer than Glen intended to stay.

Red is my favorite color. I'm not at liberty to say. Glen sat in his makeshift home office, on his cell phone, rolling his own words around in his mind and trying to understand himself—and trying not to look out his bedroom window at Christi's house. Why did he suddenly speak in code? He'd never been cryptic around her before.

Of course, he'd never wanted to reach across the table and kiss her senseless before, either.

She'd looked so perfect standing across from him, gazing into his eyes, that he hadn't been able to think about a thing, his brain had totally fogged up. Guess he should feel lucky he was able to speak at all, and that he *hadn't* acted on his impulse. Bottom line, she was the wrong woman and he had to stop thinking about her. A romantic involvement did not figure into his future. His marriage had soured him on that subject.

"Glen?" Neil prompted. "You still there?"

Thank goodness for reality!

"Just thinking," he hedged and snapped his head back from staring out the window to stare at a mouth-watering picture of pork ribs on the new calendar from Custer's Meat Market. October already? Unbelievable. "Yes, Shana gives the office space her okay. A shame you couldn't fly up there yourself."

"It's too expensive, will cut into our overhead," Neil argued, "and we'll be able to hire one fewer person."

"Saves expanding later and it's a prime location," Glen countered. "Besides, I can live off my severance."

"Yeah." Neil chuckled. "It's you high-priced executives

that suck up all the money. When you going to move up there?"

Glen glanced at a picture of himself at age nine, dressed in Irvin's army fatigues, when he'd wanted to follow in his father's footsteps and join the military. Those days seemed like a millennium ago. "The instant I complete the legal details."

"Got a place, yet?"

"No, but if I had to," he said, only half joking, "I could 'rough it' at the Four Seasons Hotel."

"Life in Miracle getting to you?"

"My dad runs a restaurant. I've pulled KP more times than I can count."

Neil laughed. "Have fun washing dishes. Let me know when everything's set up."

"Right."

Just as Glen hung up, his father appeared in the doorway. "Stark Communications shaping up?"

"Absolutely. I should be out of here by the end of the month."

"Good," Irvin said, but he frowned. "Come with me. I need help, and you need some exercise."

"You going to make me march with a full pack?"

Irvin laughed. "No, but that's not a bad idea."

Glen arched an eyebrow. His father seemed healthier, less tired, which was good, but he'd started keeping odd hours. He'd begin his day at The Pit, as usual, then just take off for two or three hours in the afternoon. Glen had no idea where his father went, but in Miracle, there weren't too many places he could go. The question was, why?

Glen followed him to the garage. Irvin stepped into The Pit's company van. "I've got to pick up turkeys from Custer's."

"That's my exercise? Lifting frozen turkeys?"

"Nope, the grass needs cutting." After saluting smartly, he backed out of the garage and drove away.

Feeling seventeen and slightly put upon, Glen returned to the house to change clothes. As he passed the kitchen door, he glanced into the backyard and stopped short. Christi stood staring down at an old lawn mower. Her hands filled her back jeans pockets, stretching the worn denim to its limits.

Glen shook his head, grabbed a red pen and circled Halloween on the calendar. Just a few more days and he'd leave Miracle and Christi's earthy attraction for good. Until then, he'd treat his feelings for her as just another hurdle to overcome.

To prove it, he hurried to retrieve the lawn mower and start on the backyard without giving her another glance.

Christi saw him right away, but pretended she hadn't. After a few minutes, her curiosity got the better of her and she looked up. Big mistake. He looked great. Tall, muscular, so full of energy, and so attractive. She still couldn't forget the kiss, nor the closeness in The Pit's kitchen, but his kindness and easy manner with Tony made it harder to ignore him. Glen the Geek was turning out to be Glen the Good.

Focus on cutting the grass.

She tried, and for the first two passes she and Glen mirrored each other, each mowing a crude rectangle around the perimeter of their respective yards. Finally she couldn't stand it any longer. She stopped, and feeling the old competitive spirit rising up, yelled, "Bet I can finish before you!"

He gave her a long look, then shook his head. "No way!"

"In a heartbeat. Loser washes and waxes the winner's car."

"*You* are not touching *my* Mercedes."

"It'll be *you* rubbing two coats of wax on *my* minivan." With a grin, she took off at a run, laughing as she mowed, feeling young and alive. Grass flew up in all directions, and twice she had to retrace her steps to catch patches she'd missed.

After twenty minutes, she wiped a dirty hand across her forehead and yelled, "Hey, slowpoke. You're slipping. I beat you by a full half a yard."

Glen finished his last pass and joined her at the back fence. "As in one and a half feet?" He arched an eyebrow. "You couldn't mean half a backyard."

"One and a half feet," she said. "Exactly eighteen in—"

He stepped closer, less than a foot away and she forgot what she was going to say. She forgot everything. The only thing on her mind was how nice it would be to kiss a nice guy, *this* nice guy. Unconsciously, she leaned forward.

"You win," he said, copying her movements. The chain link prevented leaning on the fence, so he placed his hands on the top rail in between the coiled wires. "Fastest mower in the West."

"What?" She glanced up. His eyes sparkled and his glasses reflected the late afternoon sun. "Did I hear you right?"

"I said you won. Something wrong?"

"I'm in shock. That's the first time I ever won any competition with you."

"You're memory's faulty."

"Are you kidding?" she said, momentarily forgetting about kissing him. "Thanks to you, I have 'Second Best' permanently tattooed on my forehead."

"Is that the way you saw us?"

"It was the only way *to* see it. All those debates, all those scholastic contests. Why? How did you see us?"

"As a fantastic learning experience."

"Huh? You didn't dislike me?"

"No! Why hang around with someone I didn't like?"

"Well, I sure didn't like you."

His eyes went wide. "Why?"

"Why? Because you were so confident," she said, amazed at his lack of understanding. "Did you ever falter? Did you just once doubt your capabilities?"

"About what?"

Laughing lightly, she searched his face and saw neither conceit nor arrogance, just confusion. "Oh, Glen, for a smart man, you can be really clueless."

He crossed his arms, pulling his shirt taut over his broad shoulders. Her mouth went dry.

"Are you telling me *you* had doubts?" he asked.

"All the time. Some days I took the long way home, hoping to avoid you, afraid you'd ask something I didn't know."

Disbelief filled his expression. "I had no idea."

"Yeah, right. You thrived on showing me up."

"Never. I looked forward to our debates. You always saw things so differently, and you never let me get away with anything. You picked apart my arguments in microscopic detail."

"Well, maybe," she hedged as old doubts reared their ugly heads. At age eighteen, she'd been sure of herself. After marrying Roger and allowing his demands to overshadow her needs, her goals had slipped through her fingers. She'd failed—the one thing she and Glen had never allowed themselves to even *think* about during high school. "But that was a different Christi."

"Different? How? Can't prove it by me."

"I'm fifteen years older—"

"We all are."

"Yes, but. . . ." She paused and took a deep breath. "Oh, look at our classmates, at Eleanor and Amber. They achieved their goals and managed to retain their freshness, that eagerness to tackle the world. I lost that a long time ago."

"You're wrong."

"Don't start with me, Glen," she said, wearily. "We were having a nice conversation. Don't turn it into an argument."

"I'm merely pointing out the truth. Your eyes still flash when you're challenged. Your mouth still curves up at the corners—even when you're not smiling." He cleared his throat and leaned in. "Quite frankly, I find you very fresh."

A little thrill ran through her. How long since anyone had complimented her, made her feel special? "Me?"

"You. Especially in that red dress."

He reached up to stroke her cheek and his silver-blue eyes brightened to the color of a summer sky. Christi's heart pounded, with clarity and with panic. Oh, boy, was she in trouble. He liked red, liked her in red and still thought she was fresh. What now? How did she fight him and herself?

"But, Glen, I—"

"Shhh." He cupped her face and leaned closer, tilting his head. His breath heated her cheeks. The scent of new-mown grass and his aftershave tantalized her nostrils. Her blood raced through her veins and she knew exactly what to do. He was going to kiss her again and she intended to enjoy every lip-smacking second of it. With anticipation, she closed her eyes and waited.

Chapter Five

Glen leaned closer and closer until his lips hovered over hers. Her fragrance, a mixture of roses and soap, washed over him, filling the air around them with softness. Leaves rustled. A dog barked. He leaned one inch further.

The chain link stabbed him.

"Ouch! Stupid fence."

Her eyes popped open and gleamed with unspoken questions. He backed up, putting about four feet of charged autumn air between them. What had he told himself, she was a hurdle to be overcome? Kissing her wasn't a good beginning.

"Glen?"

"That was a mistake." Her cheeks flamed. He knew he'd said the wrong thing, but saying the wrong thing was better than doing the wrong thing. "It won't happen again."

"Which?" she asked, her voice cracking. "Stabbing yourself on the fence or kissing me?"

"Blame it on gasoline fumes," he said, shoving his hands in his pockets. "For a moment there I thought we liked each other."

"You lost your head. Is that what you're saying?"

"Or maybe it's the pungent aroma of new-mown grass."

"Don't you mean *small town* grass?" She crossed her arms defensively. "What's this all about, Glen? We both know you can't wait to get out of this town."

"Absolutely," he said, clenching his teeth.

She was right. He didn't want to be here. He didn't want to be attracted to her, but he was. What about her? Could she so easily dismiss the energy between them? He could, because he'd always controlled his emotions. Not her. Christi's emotions showed clearly on her face, and she was angry.

But because he'd almost kissed her, or because he hadn't?

"I don't know," he said finally. "We don't get along. We never have—"

"So we never will?"

"I'm leaving town." He stepped back. "Soon. There's no point in pursuing an attraction."

"I wasn't pursuing anything. You leaned over to kiss me."

"You didn't stop me."

"Well, thank goodness for chain-link fences," she snapped. "If you don't mind, I'll say good-bye. I hope you and your ego are very happy together." She turned and majestically pushed the mower around the house to the garage.

Glen didn't move. The neighbors had heard every word, seen every movement—those in their backyards and others peering from behind kitchen curtains. He couldn't believe it. In his entire life, he'd never let himself get derailed from a task. Yet, just now he'd forgotten everything important: his plan for Stark Communications, his dislike of small towns, and his ex-wife's betrayal. Being with Christi clouded his judgment. Talking with her, debating like old times, kissing her—

No. He couldn't think about that again. She was intelligent, funny, firmly rooted in this small town and absolutely the wrong woman for him.

And totally impossible to forget.

After putting the mower away, he sat on the back patio, trying to clear his head. Darkness fell, bringing a cool breeze and a few twinkling stars. He stared at them, mentally calculating stellar distances, computing the time it took for the light to reach earth. He had to occupy his mind, to keep from thinking about Christi's upturned face and sweet kissable lips.

He sat there a long time, but it didn't help. There simply weren't enough stars in the sky.

After a fitful night's sleep, Irvin's drill sergeant voice jerked Glen awake "Get up! You're going to work with me."

"Gee, Dad," Glen said, his eyes barely focusing. "I'm not seventeen anymore. I can stay up late if I want."

"Get out of bed!"

"Yes, sir. What's up?"

"You need a lesson in humility," he said. "Hit the pavement. I'm leaving in five minutes."

Glen hopped out of bed. His father believed hard work cured all ills. During high school, when Glen had broken the rules, his father would roust him out of bed the next morning at four and drag him to The Pit. One Saturday, he'd stirred, baked and cut over four hundred biscuits.

What had he done to earn Irvin's anger this time?

He didn't have a clue and knew better than to ask. When his father was ready to talk, he'd do it. After they arrived at The Pit, Irvin shouldered a large bag of cornmeal from the pantry and pointed. "Get the mixer."

"What about the turkeys?" Glen groaned. "I'd rather quarter a bird than do biscuit duty."

"Cornbread," he snapped. "I didn't buy any turkeys. They were too small. Eight pounders at best."

"But cornbread?"

"I just added it to the menu."

Why? His father hated making cornbread. He baked rolls, muffins and every kind of fresh bread known to man, but he considered cornbread beneath him.

Whatever ticked him off had to be big.

After an hour, the older man unwrapped a cigar. Glen frowned. His father was smoking again? Things just got worse and worse. "You gave those up."

"Did. Your mother begged me to for years. Haven't lit one since the day she died. Figured I owed her that."

"And now?"

"You make me so mad, I don't know what I'm doing," he growled and tossed the cigar into the trash.

"About what?"

"Christi."

Glen stopped the industrial mixer and crossed his arms. "What goes on between Christi and me is our business."

"That's what you think. All of Miracle's buzzing about how you two have been acting like teenagers, yelling so the whole county can hear."

"I never yell."

"That's your problem. You keep that temper all bottled up."

"I don't have a temper."

"Oh, yes you do. Right after we moved here, you sat down right in the middle of Miracle Foods and threw a tantrum. Screamed and cried so loud you drew a crowd."

"I did not."

"That's not the only time either, but that's not the point. I'm ticked because when you finally unleashed you made her cry."

"Christi?"

"No. Lillian."

Glen had no idea what Lillian had to do with anything, but did know there was only one thing to do. "I'll apologize."

"Yes, you will. Then you'll move out."

"Move out?" Glen stepped back, surprised by Irvin's vehemence.

"The sooner the better."

"Yes, sir." Great, just great. Once again proven a failure at relationships. After all these years, he *still* couldn't get along with his own father.

"Good, now get back to work. I need four hundred squares of cornbread by noon."

"Ouch!" Lillian dropped the pan and blew on her finger.

"Mama? Did you burn yourself?" Christi hurried to her mother's side, but the older woman already had cold water running on her hand. "What happened?"

"Daydreaming, I guess. I grabbed the handle without a pot holder."

Christi searched her mother's face. She had circles under her eyes. "Mama, you look tired. Are the boys and I too much for you? We love living here, but I could rent us a house."

"You will not. I've cared for entire wards of patients that were more trouble than you."

"You were younger then."

She sighed. "Don't remind me."

Christi poured them each a cup of coffee and they sat at the kitchen table. "Well, then are you upset about what I told you yesterday? About Glen? I shouldn't have dumped that on you. I got my feelings hurt, just like in high school. I don't know why I reacted so strongly."

"Because you married a jerk who never let you be yourself."

"Mama! You said you liked Roger."

"Only because you liked him, but that man intended to live off you, honey, pure and simple."

"What? What do you mean?"

"I mean you were his meal ticket. When you had Drew and wanted to quit working, he panicked, because *he* had to get a job."

"No wonder he encouraged me in school," Christi said, dumbfounded she'd never realized the truth. "Why didn't you say something?"

"I trusted your judgment, prayed I was wrong and kept hoping Roger would mature."

"Yeah, me too."

"You're happy now, though. Except for yesterday?"

"Yes, though I hate being away from the boys all day."

"Ah, posh. They're at school most of the time."

"I know." Christi glanced at her mother, suddenly curious. "What do you do while Tony and Drew are at school?"

Lillian's cheeks turned pink. "Oh, you know . . . things."

"*Things*? Mama, what's going on?"

"Nothing's going on," she said, rather defensively. "Are you going to straighten things out with Glen?"

"There's nothing to straighten out. I got caught up in a fantasy. That's all."

"You fantasize about Glen?" Lillian rubbed her hands together. "Ooh, tell me more."

"No! I mean, I always wished we got along."

"So you'd prefer flirting rather than fighting?"

"Mama!"

"I'm just trying to understand."

"I'd like to be friends, but I guess I'll have to accept we'll always be on opposite sides. He hates this town. I love it. He wants to stay on the move. I'd be happy to nail my feet to the floor and never take another step."

"Be tough to sleep," Lillian said with a wink.

Christi laughed and draped an arm around her mother. "You're a nut, but I loved growing up with you. And I want to be like you, Mama. Just like you."

"Then apologize to Glen."

She dropped her arm and stood. "What? Why?"

"Because if you apologize first, you'll catch him off guard," she said. "Maybe then you'll get to the truth."

Christi wagged her finger. "Oh, you're clever."

Her mother handed her the phone and left the room, supposedly to give her privacy. Christi put the phone back. She couldn't call Glen. She still smarted from their encounter. Her cheeks flushed just thinking about how she'd turned her lips to receive his kiss, then acted like a witch when he'd rejected her. Her immature behavior hurt almost as much as his.

No. No point in setting herself up for more humiliation.

* * *

Thursday afternoon Glen turned to his father. "Are you going to talk to me?"

"You still here?"

"*Dad.*"

"You apologize yet?"

"Why ask me? Didn't the rumor mill tell you?"

"Don't backtalk me."

"Sorry." Glen stood and paced the small kitchen. "Truth is, I can't get up the nerve."

"Afraid you'll blow your top?"

"Yes," he lied. He feared grabbing her and kissing her again. Since their argument Saturday, he'd heard and seen nothing but Christi, Lillian, Tony and Drew. Nothing else seemed to make an impression on him.

"If you can't do it right," Irvin said, "then you'd better regroup."

"Exactly what I thought."

The fax beeped, and Glen hurried to his room. He frowned at the print and punched in Shana Matthews's number. "Hey, what's going on in Chicago?"

"Glen? Why, what's wrong?"

"We lost our office space, that's what. The Windy City Management has declared bankruptcy. All leases signed with them are null and void."

"Bankruptcy, huh? I'll check it out on this end, but I'd suggest we move on to choice number two."

Glen let out a long breath. "Shana, I—"

"Sorry, I need to go. My daughter's school is on the other line."

"Right. I'll be in touch." He hung up, punched in Neil's number and relayed the problem.

"Oh, man! Our second choice is more expensive and farther out. Glen, that's a big cut in our budget."

"I know. I'll talk to them and send you updated figures."

"Fine. I talked to Dewey and Associates about venture capital."

"Why?"

"Well, I, um, I'm thinking about getting married."

"Which means you need to safeguard your savings," Glen said with a groan—and a twinge of jealousy. "When's the wedding?"

"As soon as she says yes."

"Well, good luck. And congratulations."

He hung up the phone, grabbed a sheaf of papers and punched in another number. Their second choice had two other clients looking at the property. He had to hurry.

"Dad," he called, after a few minutes, "I've got to run to the post office. I'll see you at The Pit later."

Irvin stepped into the hall. "Something wrong?"

"A small glitch. Nothing I can't handle."

He frowned. "Guess you don't need me then. See you later."

Glen ignored his father's displeased look and hurried to the local post office before it closed.

Once he reached the counter, his irritation grew. "What do you mean it won't get there tomorrow?" he asked the postal clerk.

The woman smiled and pointed to the fine print on the sign along the wall. "We do not guarantee overnight delivery to all areas. We're a small office. One to two days."

"If I want guaranteed overnight I have to drive into Tulsa?"

"Yes, sir."

Glen considered it for a moment, but one glance at the clock told him he had no choice. With only twenty minutes before closing, he'd never get to Tulsa in time. "Small-town life," he said through clenched teeth. "Isn't it wonderful."

"I think so."

He rolled his eyes, took the receipt and left. Once back home he picked up the phone and started making calls. New office space, legal details and more venture capital kept him busy into the evening and the next day. In between calls, he worked with his father at The Pit, taking every break to phone more people and to work on his ever-evolving business plan.

By the following Friday, he'd lost feeling in his right ear from constant pressure of the telephone receiver. His vision blurred from staring at budgets, overhead costs and from reading fine print on lease agreements.

Venture capital dropped to himself only. Office space in Chicago dried to up to nothing, and Neil started talking about moving back to New York and backing out of Stark Communications entirely. Frustrated, Glen stared out his bedroom window. Christi appeared, dragging a garden hose to water the flower beds. His pulse sped up.

"No!" he yelled and tossed several paper wads at the window.

His father spoke from the hall. "What's with you?"

"My glitch went supernova," Glen snapped.

"Can I help? I've got some money put by."

Glen instantly regretted his harsh words. "No thanks, but if you can put up with me, looks like I'll have to impose on your hospitality for a little longer."

"Scrub the Halloween departure?"

"Definitely."

"Thanksgiving? Christmas?"

Glen ran a hand through his hair. "Way things are going, it may be never."

"You're too hard on yourself."

"Imagine that."

Irvin frowned. "Snide remarks aren't going to help."

"Sorry." Glen sighed. "I'm sorry we fought. I'm sorry I upset Christi and Lillian. I'm sorry about everything."

"Why don't you get out of here? Blow off steam. You've tied yourself up in knots."

"Stark Communications is my life, Dad. I can't quit now."

"Son, dreams don't come true overnight. Take a break before you overload that supersonic brain of yours."

Glen glanced outside again. The sun was about to set, but he could still make out Christi's figure. She wore a dress and no shoes. How could anyone wear work clothes to water the flowers? He frowned. "Maybe you're right."

"Tonight's Miracle High's homecoming. Why don't you go to the game?"

"Along with the rest of the town? I don't think so."

"You can't stare out that window at Christi forever."

"I wasn't staring." Glen stood and pulled the drapes closed. "I didn't even know she was out there."

"Yeah, right." Irvin paused. "Bring your work to The Pit. There'll be a big crowd tonight and I'll need the help."

"Well. . . ."

"Go on, get out of here. Enjoy yourself for once."

"I *could* use a change in scenery." He started for the door but caught his reflection in the small mirror and ran a hand over his stubbled jaw. "Think I'll shower and shave first."

"Good idea." Irvin winked. "Never know who you might see, or who might see you."

Glen groaned inwardly. "I've had a rough week, a hot shower will relax me." But even to his own ears, his words sounded lame. Could he really hope to see Christi?

"Keep telling yourself that," Irvin said. "And tell Christi hello for me." Then he walked out of the house whistling.

At the stadium, Christi sat on the concrete and wood bleachers, attempting to control her wayward children and her jumbled emotions. She intended to put sexy, arrogant, argumentative and kissable nice guy Glen out of her mind and enjoy herself. Friday night Marauder football games brought back such sweet memories. Cheering crowds, stomping feet, and an unbeatable team provided an exciting evening, reinforced of course by the band.

As a former clarinet player, tradition demanded she sit behind the musical group, so she, Tony and Drew had taken stations third row from the top. The weather was perfect. Not too warm, not too cool, and clear with a gentle southerly breeze. She rubbed her hands together in anticipation and surveyed the stands. Black and gold abounded. Miracle residents had turned out for the game dressed to the teeth in school colors.

"Mom, can I go to the snack bar?" Tony stood in front of her, both hands reaching for her fanny pack.

"It's *may* I, and no you may not." She glared at Drew before he even asked. "The game hasn't even started yet." Her sons needed a regular routine, and needed to learn how to do things on a schedule. Before they'd moved to Miracle, except for school and Cub Scouts no day had begun or ended the same. Roger's job demands had seen to that.

Plus Roger's personal demands.

"No food until after the first quarter," she repeated for the millionth time. "And only if you behave."

Both boys groaned and plopped onto the seat next to her. She wrapped an arm around each son. "Stand up," she said.

The band march onto the field. "It's time for the national anthem."

Christi belted out the Star Spangled Banner with exuberance. She'd always loved to sing, and had often wished she'd taken choral music instead of instrumental. When the band added its rendition of the state song, "Oklahoma!" she sang even louder, drawing strange looks from both her children.

"Gosh, Mom, you're weird tonight," Tony said once they sat.

"That's not Mom," Drew said, rolling his eyes. "Aliens took over her body and left this . . . creature."

Christi crossed her eyes, stuck her fingers in her ears and declared in a monotone, "Take me to your leader."

Both boys grimaced. Christi laughed and laughed and laughed, until Tony leapt to his feet. "Look, Mom, it's Mr. Stark."

She gagged on her own giggles and started to cough. *So much for putting him out of my mind.* Clearing her throat, she forced a smile on her face. "Nice to see you, Glen."

"Come sit by me," Drew insisted.

"No, me," Tony argued.

"I'm not used to being fought over," Glen said with a smile, "only being fought with."

Christi groaned inwardly, remembering the first kiss, the closeness in The Pit's kitchen, his kindness and easy manner with Tony, the near kiss and the subsequent argument. Yikes! Each encounter with this man gave her longer and longer memories. Why had he come to the game tonight?

"Christi?"

"What?"

Glen frowned. "I said, is it all right?"

Christi glanced up and was instantly mesmerized. The

field lights gleamed off his coffee-colored hair, illuminating bronze highlights. A navy pullover emphasized the blue in his eyes, and his woodsy scent tantalized her until she could barely breathe.

Her heart pounded—from her energetic singing and laughing. Okay, so she didn't believe that.

"Is what all right?" She swallowed. "All right for what?"

"Told you," Drew said. "Aliens took her over."

To her surprise, Glen laughed. "That's a good excuse. Mind if I use it sometime?"

"Sounds better than gasoline fumes," she blurted.

"A clumsy phrase snatched in the heat of battle," he admitted. "Am I forgiven?"

Clumsy? Glen had never stumbled with words in his life, except with his valedictorian speech, but that was nerves. Did she make Glen nervous? No, not possible.

Tony nudged her. "What are you two talking about?"

"I'm not sure. I think Mr. Stark is confused."

I know I am.

"Is it Friday the thirteenth or something?" Drew asked. "Because now I think aliens have taken over Mr. Stark, too." He leaned forward. "Have you seen any UFOs in your backyard, Mr. Stark?"

"No, but I'm certain I encountered a black hole when I was mowing the lawn."

"I thought all holes were black," Drew said solemnly.

Glen smiled down at him. "A black hole results from a star collapsing and becoming so dense its gravity absorbs all the light from everything around it." He turned to her, his face serious and his voice deep. "But I was referring to the pull, the draw that one intensely magnetic body can have for another."

Interest glimmered in his eyes and Christi swallowed. "A disastrous attraction."

"Exactly." He blinked, almost imperceptibly. "Get too close and you get sucked in where you don't want to be."

"I get science at school," Tony groaned. "Can we watch the game now?"

She pointed to a spot between her two sons, indicating Glen to sit, but couldn't speak a word. He was attracted to her, but considered it a mistake. Well, so did she.

Right?

"This is our first football game," Drew said.

Glen glanced at her in surprise. "You didn't watch football in the east?"

"Sure," Tony said, "but Mom said it's not regular football."

"I *said*," Christi moaned, waiting for Glen to correct her, "that they play *real* football in this part of the country."

"Your mother is right."

Christi blinked back the shock of his agreement, and tried to ignore the smoothness of his deep voice as he explained the finer points of "real" football. If she'd understood their cryptic conversation, Glen had experienced a weak moment. He was a divorced man. She was a divorced woman. Opposites attract. Only, was she negative and he positive, or the other way around?

She was positive of one thing. Knowing he found her attractive made controlling her feelings a lot more difficult. Because the more she was around Glen, the better she liked him.

In spite of comparing her to a black hole.

"Can we get something to eat now?" Drew asked after a time.

Glen stood, reaching for his wallet.

"No, Glen," Christi said, staying his hand. "I told them no food until after the first quarter." Her palm began to tingle, warm tingles of awareness. She removed her hand and rubbed it along her denim-clad thigh and tried to control herself. She was lonely. That was all. She missed male companionship. Period.

"Cooties," Tony said with emphasis.

"What?" Glen stared at her son's knowing face.

"She touched you," Drew explained. "Now you have girl cooties on you."

Christi arched an eyebrow. "Glen, I'm surprised an experienced Eagle Scout like you doesn't know about cooties."

"I just wasn't sure *who* had the cooties," he said. "Come on guys, your mom looks thirsty." He turned toward her. "Don't worry, Christi, it's the end of the first quarter."

Christi stared at the scoreboard as the three males made their way down the stairs. The first quarter had already ended? Had she been so caught up with steeling herself against Glen that she'd missed a fourth of the game? Some Marauder fan she was.

As soon as they left she realized Glen meant to pay for their snacks. She grabbed her pack and opened her wallet. Five, six, ten, seventeen; she had seventeen dollars to last until payday. Seventeen measly dollars would be pocket change to Glen. Her boys would get a taste of what real money could buy if he stuck around much longer.

She couldn't compete with that. What was the old saying? Champagne tastes on a beer budget. With her and Glen it was more like a thrift store against Tiffany's, or a stripped-down VW bug next to a deluxe Mercedes.

Which, of course, Glen owned.

Closing her eyes, she mentally cursed men, especially

Roger, who put her in this fiscal predicament in the first place.

The next thing she knew, Drew demanded, "Mom, take this drink before my hand freezes off."

Her eyes popped open and she reached to warm his fingers, but stopped short when Glen got there first.

Had that been instinctive or planned? Either way, Glen's gesture touched her heart. Anyone who took care of her sons was a hero in her book, but why Glen? What *was* happening here? Black holes. Aliens taking over her body. Glen the Geek turning into not only Glen the Good, but also Glen the Great.

Blowing out a breath, Christi faced the truth. Disastrous attraction was an understatement. She was in mortal danger of being sucked into a broken heart and didn't know how to stop it.

Chapter Six

Glen stared into her eyes, certain his confusion mirrored her own. Disastrous attraction, she'd called it, a perfect term for a black hole phenomenon, and for the irresistible pull between them.

So why did the term bother him so much?

"Mr. Stark, were you in the band?" Drew asked, slurping his soda noisily.

"Yes. I played trombone."

"Ooh, they're loud," Tony said, covering his ears.

"Very, but my dad didn't seem to mind," Glen said, smiling, "as long as I practiced in the *garage*."

Drew grinned. "What about your mom. Did she make you practice in the garage, too?"

"She did. For a while, anyway."

"Bet your mom and dad came to your concerts, too," Tony said sternly. "Our dad never came to anything. The jerk."

"Tony, that's enough," Christi said sternly.

Glen clenched his teeth, anger at Roger burning like an out-of-control oil fire. How could any man abandon his sons?

"Why didn't your mom come, too?" Drew asked. "Our mom always comes to our stuff."

"Because," Glen said, taking a deep breath as sad memories overtook him, "she passed away when I was in grade school."

"Boys," Christi said quickly, "Mr. Stark doesn't want to talk about this. Let's watch the game."

Tony peered up at him. "Did you cry?"

"Yes," Glen said.

Christi sighed. "I always wondered about that."

He faced her, surprised by the concern in her voice. Drew sat between them, but he could easily see over the small boy's head. "What are you talking about?"

"I remember you being strong, so silent, holding onto your dad's hand. I wondered if you ever had private time to grieve."

"When did you see me with my dad?"

She sighed again and turned from him. "At the funeral."

"I didn't see you."

"We, that is, some of our classmates and I came to the service. Our parents thought we were too young, but we wanted to be there. Except none of us had experienced death, so we never went inside the church—just hung out near the front door."

"Did you cry a lot?" Tony asked.

Glen turned to gaze into Tony's big brown eyes. They were full of pain and distrust. "I didn't cry at the funeral, because I wanted to be strong for my dad. I cried later. A lot."

"When you were alone," he said, as though he'd been there.

"Right." Glen looked back at Christi. "Thanks for coming."

"You're welcome."

Their gazes locked and Glen's heart thawed a little. Until that moment, he hadn't realized it was frozen. Knowing she'd cared back then, in spite of their differences, touched him.

An awkward silence hung between them for a long moment, then she turned to watch the game. Glen, feeling more relaxed than he had in years, sat back and enjoyed the company. He couldn't understand it, but he actually liked sitting between these two boys, playing the small-town family. He wasn't breathing gasoline fumes. Aliens hadn't invaded his body and he hadn't fallen into any black holes, so the fault had to be his alone.

But he felt so good, he didn't care.

During the fourth quarter, the boys entertained him with stories from school and he in turn told tales on Christi.

"Mom, did you really sprain your ankle jumping off the porch?" Drew asked.

"You told us it's dangerous to do that stuff," Tony said.

"Because I've been there," she insisted. "I don't make this stuff up, you know." She turned to Glen. "You do risky things, you take a chance of getting hurt."

"Like bungee jumping or hang gliding?" Tony asked.

Or falling in love. The thought popped into Glen's brain and he could see by the look on her face that it had crossed Christi's mind, too.

"Those, too," she said solemnly.

They'd both been hurt. No wonder their attraction was disastrous. Getting your heart broken the first time was dreadful, but taking a second chance, knowingly risking more pain, was flat insane.

So why did he keep thinking about it?

Suddenly the game was over and Christi leapt to her feet. "Playoffs, here we come!"

Glen stood along with the rest of the crowd and applauded. "You're a little premature. The season's only half over."

"Not premature. Optimistic." She flashed him a questioning look then turned to her sons. "Come on guys, time to hit the dusty trail."

"Wait a minute," Glen said, not wanting the evening to end. "How about you come with me to The Pit? Now that football season's started, the joint will be packed and I promised Dad I'd lend a hand." He turned to the boys who had suddenly gone quiet. "What about you guys, are you hungry?"

Tony got down on one knee and clasped his hands together. "Please, Mom," he begged. "I'm starving."

Drew immediately imitated his older brother. Soon the sound of pleading young boys filled the stadium air.

"I don't believe you guys," Christi said and turned to Glen. "Do *you* believe these guys?"

"They look really hungry to me," Glen said, pushing his advantage. "Come on, my treat."

The instant the words left his mouth, he knew he'd said the wrong thing again.

"No," she said quite firmly. "You've done enough."

Glen mentally kicked himself. He didn't worry about money, but he'd been there more times than he cared to count. Still, he didn't want her to decline because of the expense.

"In the name of tradition?" he suggested.

She eyed him for a long time.

"Come on," he added quickly, "The Pit is part of Miracle High football. Would you deny your sons the *complete* experience?"

She eyed him for even longer, but her face softened and in that instant, he knew she'd move heaven and earth for her boys. The thought scared him a little.

"Well, okay," she said. "But—"

Both boys visibly held their breath.

"Don't expect a treat after every game," she said.

Tony and Drew fell on her with hugs and exclamations of thanks. Glen had to bite his lip to keep from laughing.

"All right, all right," she said, kissing each boy's head. "Let go. I'm getting bruises on bruises."

"Thanks, Mr. Stark," Drew said with a grin.

"Yeah, thanks, Mr. Stark," Tony said without smiling.

The four of them started down the bleachers, but at the bottom, Tony drew him aside. "I'll pay. We don't need charity."

Surprised, Glen blinked. "Is it charity when friends get together?"

He ducked his head. "No, I guess not. But I'll still pay."

"If that's what you want, Tony. I have no problem with it."

He looked up. "You're not mad?"

"For sticking up for your mother? Never."

"Like you did for your dad when your mom, uh, you know."

"Right."

Glen took a few more steps, but Tony hung back. "Did you really cry?"

"I really did."

"I cry sometimes, too."

Realizing he was on tricky ground, Glen thought back to when he was Tony's age. "How does it make you feel when you cry? Better or worse?"

"Better, most of the time."

"Then don't stop. A good cry can be a great outlet."

"That's what Mom says, but she's a girl."

"Girl or boy, man or woman, there's no shame in crying."

"Yeah, I guess so. I'm sorry about your mom."

"Thanks," Glen said, holding out a hand. "Come on, let's get going before your mom and Drew get all the ribs."

Tony didn't take his hand, but he did walk next to him. "Let's run. Mom can eat a lot."

Glen laughed. "I think you'd better keep that to yourself."

Tony laughed, too. "Yeah, girls are sensitive about stuff like that, aren't they?"

"Son, you don't know the half of it."

Together they raced toward the parking lot.

After they'd polished off two platters of ribs, Christi leaned against the corner of The Pit's red vinyl booth and tried to remember when she'd enjoyed herself so much. Once she'd gotten past the black hole discussion, she'd almost relaxed around Glen. She'd had some tense moments when he discussed his mother's death, but was grateful he'd confessed to crying. Hearing a strong man admit to tears was exactly what Tony needed.

Since the game, he'd come to life, wolfing down ribs and laughing like a little boy should. Across the room he and Glen played a superhero video game. Tony whooped, jumped up and down and displayed more energy than Christi had seen in months. Glen laughed and Tony beamed at him. Her son needed this time with a mature man, needed it desperately.

Drew's head drooped so she pulled him close. Unlike Tony, who never gave in to fatigue, Drew knew when to call it a night.

"I think someone's ready to go to bed," Glen whispered when he returned to the booth.

Irvin walked out of the back, wiping his hands on a large apron. "Hey, buddy," he said, gazing at Drew's relaxed body. "You tuckered out already?"

"We should have left long ago," she admitted, "but Glen and Tony were having so much fun, I didn't have the heart to interrupt."

"Mom, it was an awesome game. We gotta come back here and play that again. Right, Mr. Stark?"

Glen patted Tony on the back. "Absolutely."

"That's a big affirmative," Irvin said, ruffling Tony's hair. "Makes me feel good to see a young boy eat two helpings of ribs."

Christi grinned. "Mama keeps threatening to add on another room just to store food for Tony."

"Yeah. I like to eat," Tony said, rubbing his tummy. "You cook good, Mr. Stark."

"That's Sarge to you, to both you boys."

Tony saluted. "Yes, sir."

Drew managed a tired wave.

Christi could have kissed Irvin. Only a select few were allowed to call him Sarge. To be admitted to that inner circle meant a lot to both boys, especially Tony. "Thanks, Sarge," she said, "but now it really is time to hit the dusty trail."

"Ah, Mom."

Sarge stopped Tony with a slight touch. "How you doing on your Cub Scout project?"

Tony's smile drooped. "We haven't even started."

"I thought your engineer brother was drawing up the plans."

"Drew devised spectacular plans," Christi explained with a grin. "I just don't happen to own a computer-controlled laser."

Sarge laughed. "Well, you come on over tomorrow. Glen and I will get you started."

"Yeah?" Tony said, his smile brightening.

"Affirmative," Sarge said.

Warmth spread through Christi, along with a twinge of sadness. Why hadn't Roger—just once—shown the interest in his sons these two men did? "Sarge, you're one in a million."

"So are you, Songbird," he said. "Now you better ske-daddle. I expect these boys to be bright-eyed and bushy-tailed tomorrow."

Drew giggled. "I don't have a tail."

Glen bent toward her. Christi's breath caught.

"Come on," he said, "I'll help you get Drew into the car."

"Wait, you can't carry him." Her jaw dropped as Glen lifted Drew with ease. She shut her mouth again. Grateful for the help, she gathered the boys' complimentary crayons and colorable placemats and shoved them into her jeans pocket. Tony leaned against the corner of the booth, almost asleep standing up.

"Come on, Dude." She stood and draped an arm around his shoulders. "Let's go home."

"But I'm not tired," the boy insisted through a yawn.

"Yeah, yeah," she said, ruffling his dark hair, "I've heard that before."

"Ah, Mom."

It took some maneuvering, but she and Glen got the boys into her minivan. After fastening their seatbelts, she turned to him. He stood between his car and hers, arms crossed, frowning.

"Something wrong?" she asked. The parking lot lights bounced off his wire frames and enhanced the sparkle of his eyes.

"I was wondering." He shifted his weight and dropped his arms. "What do you do when you have to handle both of them?" He indicated Tony, who'd given in to exhaustion and fallen asleep. "I can't see you carrying Tony *or* Drew."

Cars whizzed passed them, honking their horns and waving, celebrating the Marauders' victory. The cool night air blew an errant piece of paper across the concrete parking lot and somewhere a siren pierced the air. Christi barely noticed. The man across from her had captured all her attention.

"I manage," she said quietly, "but thanks for your help."

He stared for a moment, then took her left hand and rubbed the indentation where her wedding rings used to be, his thumb making slow, lazy circles on her finger. "I'm glad you came home," he said softly. "And I'm sorry about the other night."

Warm tingles raced up her arm. "I am, too, but let's not talk about it anymore."

"You were right."

Christi arched an eyebrow. "That's twice you've admitted I was right. Are you sure you haven't been possessed by aliens?"

He continued to massage her hand. "It's hard to believe that after years of fighting we'd be attracted to each other."

"Please, Glen. No more talk about black holes. I had a good time. I don't want to spoil it by arguing with you."

He raised her hand to his lips and kissed it. She blinked. Her body jolted. She blinked again.

"I have no intention of arguing. I like you, Christi, and Tony, and Drew."

"I'm, uh, glad." She swallowed hard. "Look, Glen, I appreciate your help with my sons, and the drinks and the traditional stop at The Pit, but I need to get these guys home."

"I know," he said, twining his fingers through hers, "but I don't want the evening to end."

"It has to. You were right. We want different things from life. I don't pretend to understand these feelings, and I certainly won't deny I'm attracted to you."

"Yeah?" he asked, quirking an eyebrow. "Since when?"

"Since, uh. . . ." He moved within inches and she almost forgot what she was going to say. "Oh, come on, you knew at the reunion. You smirked at me just like in high school."

"I promise, I didn't have a clue," he rasped and brought both her arms up around his neck, "but I am sure of one thing."

"What's that?" she asked breathlessly.

"There are no fences between us tonight."

Her heart skipped a beat. She licked her lips and tilted her head. "No. No fences."

His lips touched hers, gently at first, and gradually the pressure increased. But from the first moment, Christi was lost. The late hour disappeared and sunshine filled her mind. A castle glistened in the distance, and in the foreground a knight charged toward her, his sword brandished, to rescue her from . . . ?

"It's really true," she said. Her eyes remained closed and she inhaled deeply. "Brass players do make the best kissers."

"And trombone players are the best brass players."

"Mmmmm, no argument from me."

A horn honked. Christi jumped and turned toward the sound. Slowly her mental sunshine dimmed and pitch dark returned.

"This time I made the mistake," she said softly. "I guess black holes and aliens *should* be the topic of conversation."

"Christi, it's one kiss. It doesn't mean—"

"Doesn't mean commitment?" She raised her hand to stop his protest. "Don't you see? This black hole engulfs more than just you and me. I have to consider Tony and Drew. They're beginning to like you, but what happens when you leave? It will be their father all over again. I won't let that happen, Glen. I *can't* let that happen."

"Christi, wait, please."

"No, I can't. It's better this way."

After a great deal of fumbling, she reached into her pack, found her keys and managed to get into the car. Through tears, she started the engine and sped out of the parking lot.

She didn't dare look back, because he'd be there, watching her. Arms crossed, leaning against his Mercedes, he'd look more handsome, more *attractive* than any black hole thought about being. Succumbing to his pull wasn't an option. She couldn't give in, no matter what.

Oh, but she wanted to—more than anything she'd ever wanted in her whole life.

Chapter Seven

Glen watched Christi's minivan until her taillights faded into red pinpoints. Still, he couldn't turn away. Black hole was an understatement. He crossed his arms to calm the rapid rise and fall of his chest, but failed.

He had to leave Miracle and soon. He had no time for a romantic interlude. Besides, he simply wasn't good at relationships. After his wife left him, he'd vowed to never get involved again. It hurt too much when he failed. Better to stick to business. *That* he knew how to handle.

Disappointed he'd let Christi get under his skin again, he drove home, quietly let himself into the house, and sat at his computer until the wee hours of the morning. After that, he called the airlines to book a flight to Chicago to once again look over office space.

Then and only then did he sleep.

He awoke the next morning to the sound of children's laughter. Raising up on one elbow, he stared out his bedroom window to see Tony and Drew talking to his dad. What in the world? Oh, the Cub Scout project. Great, after only a few hours of sleep, he'd probably saw off a finger.

He dressed quickly, grabbed a mug of coffee from the kitchen and headed into the backyard. "What's going on?"

"Hi, Mr. Stark," Tony said with a smile.

Glen paused, surprised. Tony had spoken first. Usually he let Drew handle the greetings. Christi had warned Glen the boys might get attached to him. He'd never considered it, because he'd never been relaxed around kids.

He resolved to remain as neutral as possible.

" 'Bout time you rolled out of the sack," Irvin said. "One more minute and I'd—" He stopped in mid-sentence, his gaze focused on the side yard.

Christi and her mother rounded the corner of the house. Apparently the boys had hopped the fence while the two women had properly walked around the block. Christi, clad in her usual jeans and T-shirt, smiled hesitantly. Lillian, in a hot pink pants outfit, smiled broadly.

"Good morning, Irvin," she said sweetly.

"Well, good morning, Lillian. Don't you look pretty today."

"Thank you," she said, her cheeks reddening slightly.

Glen's jaw dropped, not because Lillian blushed, but because his father's face lit up. If he smiled any broader, his face would split in two.

Could his dad and Christi's mom . . . ? No! The saccharine-tainted Miracle air must have warped his brain. Lillian Pierce had been their neighbor for over twenty years. Of course his dad would greet her pleasantly.

Drew tapped his arm, interrupting his thoughts. "Mom says you're an engineer. I'm going to be an engineer someday. Mom says I have a knack for it."

"You do?" Glen asked, curious how Christi defined "knack."

"Yeah." Drew sighed. "But I can't get the remote controls to work. They operate on infrared. That's why you don't need wires from the remote to the TV."

"You don't?" Glen asked, hoping Drew would continue. He did.

Drew began drawing pictures in the air, first a long rectangle, then several smaller ones inside. "See," he said, indicating a strip near the top of his air diagram, "the IR pulse goes out there and meets the sensor on the cable box or TV or VCR. If you block either one it doesn't work."

"Interesting. Then what happens?"

"Well, it's hard to explain," Drew said, frowning, "but since you're an engineer, you might understand."

Glen bit his lip to keep from smiling, and absorbed every word of the boy's explanation of the workings of a remote control. His descriptions were vivid and detailed, and other than reversing a couple of functions, he pretty much had it nailed.

No doubt about it, Drew had a "knack."

Christi put a hand on her hip. "If you two are finished solving the mysteries of the electronic universe, we need to get started on this birdhouse."

Drew frowned. "Ah, Mom, it's guy talk."

"Well, this 'girl' says it's time to get to work. Glen, is everything ready to go?"

"Dad," he asked, "we ready to get started?"

"You go ahead," Irvin said, never taking his eyes from Lillian. "I'll be along in a minute."

"Right. Come on guys."

Tony, Drew, and to Glen's surprise, Christi followed him to the garage. His father had backed out the Mercedes and the van and set up two makeshift workbenches from saw-horses and plywood. The birdhouse had been laid out and—thank goodness—the parts were already pre-cut.

At least he wouldn't saw off any fingers.

Unfortunately Christi moved next to him to examine the parts and his brain began to fog. Sweat beaded on his forehead, too, so he blinked rapidly and tried to concentrate.

"It looks like we need to pre-drill the holes," Christi said.

"Looks like." He glanced out into the back yard. What had happened to his father?

"Drew, come read us the instructions," she said. "Glen, you handle the drill."

Tony frowned. "Ah, I wanted to handle the drill."

"No whining, young man," Christi said. "Let the adults get you started, then you can have your turn. Right, Glen?"

He inhaled deeply. She smelled really fresh this morning.

"Glen?" she prompted.

"What?"

"What's the matter?" she asked, waving a hand in front of his face. "You miss your morning coffee?"

Finally, he snapped back to reality. "Yes. No. I mean, I was up late struggling with budgets."

"Problems?"

"Normal business ups and downs."

"Then can we get started?"

How he managed to concentrate, he didn't know, but he and the boys, under Christi's supervision, managed to drill holes, nail three sides together and screw on the perch. Tony handled a drill well, but Drew smashed the nails in with the fewest blows.

"Leverage," he explained, as if all eight-year-olds had a complete understanding of physics. "Tony's bigger, but I hold the hammer different and get more power."

Christi smirked. "That's my boy."

"Well, all that's left is the staining," Glen said when they finished. "How about it boys? You game?"

Tony rubbed his stomach. "I'm hungry."

"Me, too."

"It's still early, yet." Glen glanced at his watch, hardly able to believe he'd spent nearly four hours with Tony, Drew and Christi. He would have sworn only a few minutes had passed.

"Thanks for your help," Christi said quickly, "but we need to go."

She shot him a pleading look. His heart stopped and all logical thought left his brain. He was falling for her. She and her sons had captured his heart and there wasn't anything he could do about it.

Except be scared to death.

Drew tugged on his sleeve. "Hey, Mr. Stark, are you any relation to Iron Man?"

Grateful for the interruption, Glen flexed his muscles. "I'm his nephew, Steel Man."

Christi choked and covered her mouth with her hand. "You know who Iron Man is? I mean, you read comic books? You don't consider them beneath you?"

"Are you kidding? I used to tell people Iron Man was my rich uncle. You know, Tony Stark, billionaire industrialist, secret identity of Iron Man." He crossed his arms. "*And*, I have the *first* Iron Man comic."

"Wow!" Both boys turned so quickly they collided with each other. "Can we see it? Please! Please!"

"Christi?" Glen watched her face. "Do you mind?"

Tony spoke so quietly Glen almost didn't hear him. "Please, Mom. Iron Man rules."

She nodded and Tony turned to Glen. "Mr. Stark, you are so cool."

"Because I read comics?"

"Sure. Mom keeps saying what a geek you were and, well, geeks don't read comics."

"Thanks."

"For what?"

Glen gazed into Tony's eyes and for the first time saw no hint of hesitance. He couldn't believe how much it meant for Tony to like him. "For saying I'm cool. Geeks get tired of being called geeks."

"Really?"

"Really," he said, glancing at Christi. "We have feelings just like everyone else."

Her eyes widened and Glen barely heard Tony's response.

"Yeah," he said softly.

Glen moved to the attic access at the back of the garage, and after a couple of minutes, located a huge box marked "Comics." From the box he pulled a locked metal tin, his makeshift safe for his precious collectibles, and brought out the first edition comic. Protected by a plastic cover, he held it up for each boy to examine.

"Awesome," Drew whispered.

"Yeah," Tony agreed, "but we can't read this one, can we?"

"Sorry." Glen put it away, and pulled out the large box. "But these you can."

"Wow!" Tony opened the lid and grabbed a handful. "There must be a million in here!"

"Close to it, I'm sure. Take them home if you want."

"We can keep them?"

"Well, no, but you can borrow them."

"Like at the library?"

"Exactly," Glen said and grinned. "Consider me your personal comic book library."

Both boys scrambled to pick out their favorites and Glen closed up the attic access. After a few steps, he stopped dead in his tracks.

Drew's big little voice echoed in the small garage. "Wow, Tony. If Mr. Stark married Mom, then you'd be Tony Stark. And *you* could be Iron Man."

Christi gasped.

"Shut up, dweeb," Tony commanded in a strained voice. "Just *shut up*."

Drew's words stabbed right to Glen's heart. This was exactly what Christi had meant. He'd been an idiot not to see it. These boys had a father who ignored them. Christi's father was no longer alive, so they had no male role model. The instant he and Irvin had showed them some consideration, they latched onto it.

Glen fled into the house through the door to the kitchen. He heard Christi follow him.

Again, he stopped dead in his tracks. Christi bumped him from behind, but he barely felt the jolt. The sight in front of Glen numbed him completely.

His father and Lillian were kissing!

"What in the world is going on in here?" he demanded.

"Mama!" Christi said over his shoulder.

Lillian gasped and jumped back, her cheeks apple red. Irvin wore an expression Glen could only classify as sheepish. For a moment no one said anything. Then all four spoke at once.

"Son, I can explain."

"Christi, Irvin and I are—"

"Are what, Mama?"

"Yeah, what?" Glen demanded.

Lillian put a hand to her cheeks. "I told you we should have told them right away."

"Told us what?" Christi asked.

Suddenly Drew burst into the room and hugged Irvin. "I saw you kiss Grandma. Does this mean you're my Grandpa now?"

"No!"

Glen and Christi blurted the word together, and stared at each other. He watched her eyes flash with anger, as if she blamed him. The walls closed in. All the small-town holds he'd tried to escape, the bad memories of the past flooded his brain. He clenched his teeth. "I'd like to speak to my father—alone."

"Yes, I think that's a good idea," Christi said stiffly. "Come on boys, let's go home." She headed for the front door, and turned. "Coming, *Mother*?"

Lillian hesitated, glanced from Christi to Irvin and sighed deeply. "Do I have a choice?"

Glen watched them go and turned to his father. As if he were the parent and Irvin the son, Glen crossed his arms. "You have a lot of explaining to do."

"What's between me and Lillian is my business, not yours."

"How could there be anything between you and Lillian?" Glen ran a hand through his hair. This couldn't be happening. His father and Lillian? They were more opposite than he and Christi. "I mean, you were devoted to Mom."

"Yes, I was," Irvin said, his voice heavy with sadness, "and I've been alone ever since—over twenty years."

Glen dropped into a kitchen chair. "You're lonely?"

"Yes. For a partner, the life-long kind."

"Dad, you're almost sixty," Glen groaned. "A man your age doesn't . . . doesn't."

"Doesn't fall in love? Well, you're wrong. I'm fifty-eight and that's just what I am, in love—with all that implies," he said, waggling his eyebrows. "So get used to it." Then he strode to his bedroom whistling.

Glen shuddered. He had to get out of this town before he lost his sanity entirely, but first, he'd break up his father's romance. After that he'd find an apartment in Chicago and forget all about Christi *and* her sons.

And keep his mind where it belonged—where he felt safe—on business.

The moment Christi reached home, she sent the boys out to the yard to play and dragged her mother into the kitchen. "You want to explain what you were doing plastering yourself all over that man?"

Lillian squared her shoulders. "That man has a name."

"Fine, then explain why you were hanging all over Irvin."

"I wasn't hanging. I was kissing him."

Christi collapsed onto a kitchen chair. "But Mama, he's all wrong for you. What about Daddy? You two were so happy."

"Yes, we were. Your father was prime husband material. He had a good job, never raised his voice or his hand to me, and never looked at another woman. I loved him dearly."

"But?"

"But, I've been alone a long time. So has Irvin. We care about each other."

"Then why hide it?"

"Because of you and Glen."

Christi nearly choked. "Me and Glen?"

"Irvin wanted to tell Glen right away, but I stopped him. You'd just moved back to town and I knew you'd be upset about any more changes in your life. Besides, you've never really liked Glen." She paused. "Right?"

"We've never been friends," Christi said dully.

"Obviously. The whole neighborhood heard you two arguing."

"The point is," Christi said, taking her mother's hand, "you're making a mistake. Irvin's wrong for you. Don't do what I did. Don't get involved with the wrong man."

"I am involved, and he's the right man, so get used to it," Lillian said and waltzed out of the room.

Christi hurried into her private bathroom and turned on the faucet. Tears flowed with the water. She liked Irvin. He had good qualities, but her mother was special.

Irvin was a crusty old drill sergeant. For goodness sake, he had a tattoo!

She had to split them up. No way would she let her mother be hurt the way she'd been. First thing tomorrow, she'd talk to Glen and demand his assistance. Maybe together, they could develop a strategy.

Sunday afternoon Christi reached for the phone to call Glen, but stopped. She didn't know what to say. How could she ask him to break up her mom and his dad without slandering Irvin? She returned to folding the laundry and tried to plan an approach.

A new thought struck her. What if her mother and Irvin got married? Where would they live? Where would she and the boys live? She sighed and stared at the receiver, uncertain what to do. Was she being selfish? Did she want to split the couple apart just to keep a roof over her head and a free baby-sitter?

Could she be that petty?

Before she could answer herself the doorbell rang. Drew rushed out of his room and ran to the door. "It's Grandpa and Glen!"

Christi bit her lip. "No, it's Sarge and Mr. Stark."

"Ah, Mom, Sarge kissed Grandma. That makes him part of the family, doesn't it?"

"Shut up, dweeb," Tony said from the hallway. "He has to marry Grandma to be part of the family."

Drew shrugged. "Okay, I'll ask him."

"No, Drew," Christi said gently. "Just let them in." Unable to help herself, she straightened her clothes. The weather had turned cool, an autumn crispness in the air, so she'd donned an old pair of sweats. Unconsciously she wished she had time to change into something less small town mom-ish.

Lillian entered the room and Christi stepped into the kitchen to watch her greet Irvin. Once the older couple saw each other, they lit up. Christi sighed. This was going to be harder than she thought.

"Hi, Sarge," she said, strolling into the foyer. "Hello, Glen."

"Songbird." Irvin leaned over and kissed her cheek. "You're looking lovely today."

Glen rolled his eyes and crossed his arms.

"Thanks," she said. "I think the boys want to show you their birdhouse. We stained it after, well, yesterday."

Tony and Drew took their grandmother and Sarge by the hand, and dragged them to the garage. Christi motioned to Glen. "I need to talk to you."

"I hope you're against this . . . arrangement," he said stiffly.

"Yes. You?"

"Absolutely."

"So what do we do about it?"

"I'm going to talk Dad into going to Chicago with me."

For some reason Christi's heart sank. "You are?"

"Absolutely."

"You said that already."

"And I meant it."

"When?"

He stared at her, his gazed roaming over her from head to foot. "When, what?"

Her heart thumped. "When are you leaving?"

He sagged slightly. "I don't know."

"Business problems?"

"I don't suppose you have a couple hundred thousand dollars laying around just waiting to be invested?"

She blinked. "What?"

"Nothing. So, what do we do about the odd couple?"

"I've talked to Mama."

"I've talked to Dad."

"And?"

Sarge and Mama reappeared. "*And* we've talked it over," he said. "Now that you kids know how we feel, we're going public."

"Oh, great," Christi said, but out of the side of her mouth muttered to Glen, "All right, genius, do something."

"Like what?" he muttered right back.

"He's your father."

"Well, she's your mother."

"You're a big help." Christi frowned. "Are you sure, Mama? Gossip is pretty rough in this town."

"After the show you two put on, we're nothing."

"Us?" Christi stalled a blush. "We haven't done anything."

"Arguing over the back fence," Lillian said. "Going to the football game together—"

"We didn't go together," Glen insisted.

"Kissing in The Pit parking lot," Sarge added.

"We didn't," Christi began. "Oh, yeah. We did."

Lillian patted Christi's cheek. "For two people who claim they don't like each other, you certainly spend a lot of time smooching in public."

"Exactly what does going public mean?" Glen asked quickly.

Christi sighed with relief at the change of subject. "Yes, what does that mean?"

"It means you baby-sit while we go out on the town," Sarge said.

"In this town? There's nothing to go out on," Glen quipped.

Irvin waggled his eyebrows. "We'll think of something."

Glen groaned.

Christi blushed right along with her mother. "What does *that* mean?"

Glen shook his head. "I'm not sure I want to know."

"You two old fogies have fun," Lillian said smiling. "We'll be back when you see us walking up the drive."

Over the next several days, Glen watched his father act more and more like a lovesick schoolboy. Irvin grinned, made silly jokes, and spent big bucks on flowers. To make matters worse, the town loved it. Everywhere Glen went, people smiled, waved or shook his hand, all eager to recount some story of seeing Irvin and Lillian together.

What sent him around the bend, though, was Lillian's insistence that the two families spend time together. The six of them would have dinner at her house, then Glen would have to watch Lillian and his father make goo-goo eyes at each other. Yuk! Being around Christi just made things worse, because he'd catch himself wanting to make goo-goo eyes at her.

Man!

The day after Halloween, he sat staring at the television trying not to watch or listen to his father cuddle with Lillian—and trying harder not to stare at Christi while she sat at the desk opposite him quietly paying bills—and his patience ran out.

"I'm going home," he whispered.

"Oh, no you don't," she muttered, scribbling some numbers on a piece of scratch paper. "Not unless you take *him* with you."

"*He* has a name," Glen said stiffly, keeping his voice low.

"Okay, you can't go home until you take *Mr. Stark* with you."

"What's set you on edge?" He glanced at the figures. "Too much month at the end of your money?"

"Like you've ever been there," she said in a harsh whisper, and shoved her checkbook under a mound of papers. "Don't pry into my life, Glen. Your father's done enough."

"What does that mean?"

"He's got Mama all messed up, turned her into a lovesick teenager," she said, her whisper taking on a crisp, terse tone. "It's sickening."

"Then do something about it."

"Me?"

"Yes, you," he insisted, his frustration sharpening his own voice. "We agreed, didn't we?"

"We agreed something needs to be done about your father."

"You think it's Dad's fault?"

"*He* approached *her*. My mother would never chase a man."

Irvin spoke up. "Will you two pipe down? We're trying to watch a show here."

"Stop pretending, Dad," Glen snapped. "The movie's been over for twenty minutes."

Lillian giggled.

"You see!" Christi leapt to her feet and dragged Glen into the kitchen. "My mother giggled. A fifty-plus woman giggling. It isn't dignified."

"You're crazy."

"Watch it, Einstein," she warned. "You're treading on thin ice here."

"Why do we always wind up in the kitchen?"

She stopped and stared. "What?"

"Every time we get into an argument, we wind up here in the kitchen."

"You got a problem with kitchens?" she asked, raising an eyebrow.

"Not particularly," he said, eyeing her. "You?"

She swallowed visibly, and he wondered if she was thinking about The Pit's kitchen, and him tying her apron. He certainly was thinking about it. All the time.

"Not at all," she murmured and turned to run her hand over the counter. "I always feel at home in the kitchen."

Not exactly the response he wanted, or was it?

"But you hate to cook," he said, unsure why he cared, only knowing he did.

She laughed. "Why do you remember that?"

"Mind like a steel trap," he said, tapping his temple. "I never forget anything."

"Roger never stepped beyond the refrigerator. So, when I couldn't handle the arguing anymore, I retreated to the kitchen, to safety."

Been there. Done that. More than once. He and his ex had drawn battle lines, too, only Glen had retreated to his office—completely out of the house. Fresh pain at failing as a husband poured through him.

Time to change the subject.

"Safety in the kitchen, huh? For me it was always a punishment. In, fact, since I've been back, I've spent a lot of afternoons—" Man! "What does Lillian do while the boys are at school?"

"What? Things. Probably rests for the afternoon on-slaught of two energetic boys. I don't know. Why?"

He couldn't believe he hadn't seen it before. "Since I arrived in Miracle, Dad's been slipping away from The Pit in the afternoons. And I just now realized he always got back about the time school let out."

"You mean they've been spending their afternoons to-gether all this time?"

"August to November," Glen said. "And who knows how long before?"

"I think we may have underestimated their affection."

Irvin and Lillian appeared in the doorway. "My ears are burning, Lil," he said. "How about yours?"

Lillian shook her head. "Gossip right here in my own house. Guess we'd better tell them."

He nodded. "I agree."

"Tell who what?" Christi asked.

"We've decided you're right," Irvin said. "Going public has caused a lot of talk and we want it to stop."

"You're splitting up," Christi said, and shot Glen a look of triumph.

He almost returned it until he saw his father grin and take Lillian's hand. "Dad?"

"No," Irvin said and grinned. "We're getting married."

Chapter Eight

"**M**arriage? Are you kidding?" Christi asked, stunned.

"Of course we aren't kidding," her mother said. "As soon as arrangements can be made, we're getting hitched."

"Well, that's great," Glen said, his eyes not quite registering the happiness of his words. "Congratulations."

"Yeah, congratulations," Christi echoed and shot him a look of panic. He nodded toward the garage, and once Sarge and Mama left the room, she hurried to meet him there. "Now what?"

"They're bluffing, they have to be," Glen said, frowning.

"And if they aren't?"

"I don't know," he said, running a hand through his hair. "Talk to her, stall—and keep an eye on these *arrangements.*"

"And what will you be doing?"

"The same."

"Okay." They shook hands on their secret marriage-busting pact, and Christi almost swooned. "I'll keep in touch."

"Yeah," he said huskily, "you do that."

Sarge and Glen left soon after that, so Christi started in on her mother, but Lillian was adamant. "We're not getting any younger," she said. "Why wait?"

Christi brought up a lot of reasons, but her mother shot each one down. Finally, she backed off, thinking maybe if she ignored the problem it would go away.

That worked, until she overheard her mother making a doctor's appointment. Christi hurried to work, into Eleanor's office to use the phone in private and punched in Glen's number.

"Yes?" he asked, picking up after the first ring.

"Marriage alert, marriage alert," she said softly.

"Christi? What's wrong?"

"Mama's going to get a blood test today."

"Uh-oh."

"Yes, uh-oh. We have to talk about how to stop this— right now. Can you meet me somewhere?"

"Where can we go in this town and be alone?"

She blew out an exasperated breath. "Nowhere."

"Better go public then."

"Okay. Meet me for lunch at the Route 66 café, at one."

"Will do."

The time dragged until lunch. When she finally got to the café, she was more than a little anxious—about her mother, of course. Seeing Glen had nothing to do with it.

So why, though she sat on a high stool at the counter with her back to the door, did her body start tingling from head to toe the exact moment Glen walked into the café? Oh boy, was she in trouble. Swiveling toward him, she smiled and tried to keep the excitement out of her voice. "Hey."

"Hey, yourself," he said and sat next to her. "What's up?"

"The sky," she quipped, trying to slow down time, make this meeting last longer.

"Very funny."

"Not much on small talk, are you?"

"Never was."

"Then how'd you manage that speech at the reunion?"

"Practice."

"Practice?"

"That's right."

She rolled her eyes. "Getting information out of you is like pulling teeth."

The waitress handed him a menu. "You want to order now, or fight first?"

"Order," Glen said. "I argue better on a full stomach."

Unable to help herself, Christi looked him over, hoping to find a flaw, a reason to stop wanting to be near him.

No such luck.

Dressed in light gray gabardine slacks, a navy blue starched dress shirt, black belt and shoes, he looked crisp, professional, and very "near-able."

"Tell me something," she said.

"The earth is ninety-three million miles from the sun."

"I meant something I didn't already know, Wise Guy."

"Shana Matthews has a nine-year-old daughter."

Jealousy arrowed through her. "Who's Shana Matthews?"

"A colleague."

"She divorced?"

"Who knows."

"She's your friend and you don't know if she's divorced?"

"I met her after she became a single parent. I never asked how she got that way."

"What do you talk about with your friends?"

"Work."

"Only work?"

"Right."

"If that's true, how did you manage to fall in love and get married?" She bit off a grin. "I know, your wife proposed."

He reared back and peered at her. "How did you know?"

Aha! "Female intuition."

"Bunk."

"Oh, please, don't go all technical on me."

"Did you call me down here to fight or—"

"Shhhhh." Christi sipped her water and glanced around. "Not so loud. You want to spread gossip?"

He turned to the five people in the café. "Anybody here care why Christi and I are sitting at this counter?"

"No!" came the resounding reply.

He shrugged. "Fire away."

"Don't you care what people think?"

"Not anymore."

"Well, I do. I have two sons to think about."

"Look, Christi. You never used to beat around the bush with me. Say what you want to say and get it over with."

"You're right. I want to you to leave town."

"That's not a secret."

"I mean, now, tomorrow. And take Sarge with you."

"What are you talking about?"

She sighed. "It's the only thing I can think of." *To get*

rid of Sarge, and you. "These past few days I've been waiting for them to argue, hoping I could jump in—"

"And point out how different they are?"

"Yeah, like us."

He knit his dark eyebrows. "We aren't so different."

"Night and day. Black and white."

"More like red and yellow."

"Excuse me?"

"Red and yellow. Picture the color wheel. The three primary colors, red, blue, yellow form a triangle. Although in the visible light spectrum, they're part of a linear—"

"Glen!"

"What?"

"I'm perfectly aware of the relative positions of the colors of the visible light spectrum, linearly and on the color wheel. What's your point?"

"We're not diametrically opposed, but juxtaposed against the third point of the triangle."

"For goodness sakes."

He stopped, stared, and turned his attention to the clock on the wall. "Sorry. I get carried away, sometimes."

"I wish you would."

"Christi, that is such an old joke."

"Well, what I have to say isn't funny. Our parents are going to get married sooner than we think. Three days after the blood test, they can get the license."

"Relax. Dad hates needles. Said he got stuck too often in the Army. He'll put it off awhile."

"That's not enough. We need to come up with a way to show them, to prove to them. . . ." She glanced at her watch. "Oh, rats, I have to get back to work. I'll call you later."

He raised an eyebrow. "And spread gossip?"

"Why are you being so difficult?"

"*I'm* being difficult?"

"Okay, okay, I apologize for any aspersions I may have cast on your father's character."

"*May* have cast?"

"Look, I said I'm sorry." Exasperated, she planted one hand on her hip. "Do you have many friends?"

"Not too many."

"Didn't think so." She paid her check and attempted to get off the stool and make a graceful exit.

The stool had other ideas.

Her skirt caught on a ragged metal edge and she stumbled into Glen, winding up nose to nose.

Wow! She stared into his silver-blue eyes, mesmerized until she couldn't breathe. And she didn't dare move, because his very kissable lips were less than an inch away and the temptation to taste them was just too great.

To her great comfort—and disappointment—he didn't move either, so for a long, delectable moment they remained a whisper apart, sharing the same warm air.

Christi's heart nearly pounded out of her chest.

Finally, Glen cleared his throat and set her away from him. "I'll, uh," he croaked, "I'll talk to you later."

Next thing she knew, she was out on the sidewalk.

Wow! Double and triple wow! That man was beyond attractive, he was captivating, more than her ex-husband ever thought about being. Which meant she didn't dare allow herself to be drawn in—no matter how nice a guy he might be.

She'd traveled that road before and it only led to pain. No, she wouldn't take that trip again. Nor would she allow her mother to do so with Irvin. Not in a million years.

* * *

Glen either e-mailed or phoned Christi every day for the next several days. He saw her, too, because he couldn't keep from looking out the window, but Stark Communications kept him from physically being with her. Which was good, because since their meeting at the Route 66 café, he needed to put distance between them. Talking with her was distracting enough, but when he was in her presence, he couldn't think about anything except how complete she made him feel.

That was the problem. He felt too—too much—when he was around her, and it made him want to do strange things like kiss her in public. Unacceptable. No matter how good she made him feel, or how much he enjoyed making her laugh, he wasn't going to spend any more time with her than necessary.

Yet, he couldn't avoid her. They needed to get together and come up with a plan, especially now. Early this morning, his father had gone to the doctor for *his* blood test.

The phone rang and he hesitated. Was it her? Could he control himself, or once he heard her silky voice, would he start babbling like a public television science special?

The phone rang again.

"Answer that, will ya?" Irvin yelled from the other room.

"Yes?" he said after snatching up the receiver.

"Hey, I married an heiress!"

"Neil?" Glen blew out a breath.

"Of course. I did it, buddy. I'm a newlywed."

"Congratulations, but I thought the wedding was set for after the first of the year."

"We eloped," he said, laughing. "Crazy for two people in their thirties, but once we got the blood tests we just did it."

A lump formed in Glen's throat. He'd put off his wedding four times due to his work schedule. Not once had he considered eloping. Now, his best friend had done so.

Would his father do so as well?

He balled up a piece of paper and threw it against the window. It was too dark to see anything but porch lights and street lamps, but he knew Christi and her mother sat out there somewhere. Pesky chain link fences. If everyone put up solid wood ones, neighbors wouldn't go falling in love with each other.

"So what's this about an heiress?" he asked.

"Not really an heiress. Her aunt left her some money."

"Some?" Glen asked, his hopes mounting. "Enough to live on while we get Stark Communications off the ground?"

"You got it. Coupled with my severance we should be able to hold out for a year. Plus she has a good job."

"Yes! Stark Communications is back on course."

"I'm still talking to Dewey. Extra capital never hurt."

"You keep talking, Neil. And kiss the bride for me."

Neil chuckled. "For me, too. Talk to you soon."

"Soon." Excited his dream wasn't dead after all, Glen hung up and called Christi. "Meet me at The Pit in half an hour."

"Yes, sir," she snapped. "Shall I bring my steno pad?"

"Oh, come on. You know what I mean. I've got good news."

Her voice brightened. "Yeah?"

"Definitely. Be there or be square."

"Oh, Glen, you are such a geek."

"Hey, geeks will inherit the earth. Or at least own the biggest chunk."

She laughed. "You're nuts. See ya."

He hung up and glanced out the back window, trying to

tell what she was doing. It wasn't quite nine, which meant Tony was fighting going to bed. Glen could picture both boys begging for another book, five more minutes of TV, all the things kids did to stall. If only he could be there.

No! He was kidding himself. They got along because he saw them bits at a time. He didn't have the stamina to raise them, to teach them to survive or to help suffer their disappointments.

If Irvin married Lillian, though, he could be a bigger part of the boys' lives.

Stop thinking like that.

Irvin and Lillian were as opposite as . . . he smiled. What had he spewed at the café? Juxtaposed against the third point of a triangle? His smile drooped. Christi was the only person who realized he resorted to science talk when he got nervous.

Keep your mind on business.

Frustrated, he jerked the drapes closed. "I'm going out, Dad," he yelled on his way to the garage.

"Be careful," Irvin yelled back.

Glen shook his head. His father had no idea how appropriate that parental standard was.

"Well?" Christi asked when he arrived at the back door of The Pit. She stamped her feet. A cold north wind whipped down the alley. "Good ol' Oklahoma fall," she said, "seventy in the afternoon, thirty at night. The temperature drop is killing me."

"Why didn't you wait inside?"

"I thought this was a clandestine meeting," she said, the corners of her mouth curving upward. "Real spy stuff."

"Fun, isn't it?"

"Yeah."

He opened the door to the kitchen. Warmth blasted them

and a young man dressed in a long-sleeved white shirt and black pants stepped into their path. "I'm sorry, you can't . . . oh, hi, Mr. Stark. I didn't know you were coming. Is there a problem?"

Glen stared at the pimple-faced youngster. His nametag stated assistant manager, but he couldn't be more than nineteen. "No problem. Dad just asked me to check some paperwork."

"Okay. Hi, Mrs. Farley. How are you?"

She smiled. "Fine, Joey, thanks. Looks like you're doing a great job."

"Gee, thanks."

Glen watched the boy turn five shades of red just because Christi smiled and knew *exactly* how he felt. He'd started flushing out in the alley.

He spotted a few broken-down boxes in the corner. "What's that stuff doing there?"

"Miracle Leasing keeps thinking someone will rent that office space, so they cleaned up a little. I told them I'd put the boxes out with our trash. Is that all right, Mr. Stark?"

Glen raised an eyebrow in amazement. Why did he have such an easy time understanding the rest of the world, and such a difficult time figuring out Miracle? The Pit was popular because Irvin hired local teens. He not only hired them, he trained them and trusted them with responsibility.

"You did just fine, Joey. Thanks. Think I'll go check it out. You game, Christi?"

"Sure. I haven't been up there since the Little Princess Dance Studio went out of business."

"Be careful," Joey warned and returned to the dining area.

Taking Christi's gloved hand—just to be careful—they climbed the steep stairs together. Noises from The Pit—

teenagers laughing, video games blasting, and the jukebox blaring—filtered up through the walls and the floor.

When they reached the top, pitch black greeted them. Glen fumbled for a light, found the power main and threw the switch. Light splashed over the room.

"Man!" His voice echoed. "This place is huge."

Strolling to the bank of floor-to-ceiling windows, he peered down to the street. He could see the awning of Miracle Tours, the shield-shaped sign for the Route 66 café, and about ten other shops. If he squinted, he could almost make out the glow of the Arkansas River on the northern edge of town.

"You took dance lessons here?" he asked.

"In that corner," she said, indicating a wood floor and two walls of mirrors. "But we came up the other staircase, you know the one on the corner that opens onto Route 66."

Glen switched his gaze to the corner where Main Street intersected Route 66. "They must have knocked out some walls."

"Not recently," Christi insisted. "Eleanor's mother wouldn't allow it."

"But this was a warehouse originally. Makes sense the upstairs would be one big room."

She shrugged. "So, what's the good news?"

"Ah." He led her over to the wood floor, which looked cleaner than the rest and sat. "Join me."

"Why? Are you coming apart?"

Glen groaned. "Christi, that is such a horrible joke. Now, please, sit and talk to me."

She didn't. Instead, she grimaced at herself in the mirrors, turned left, right, and all the way around. "Geez, I look awful. Why didn't you tell me I look awful?"

He sighed. "Women."

"Don't give me that tone, Glen Stark. I look like an old maid school teacher and you know it."

He looked at her, really looked. Her coat was at least ten years old. Purple sweats peeked out from beneath the hem, along with a pair of scuffed running shoes. But her face glowed. Her hair sparkled in the overhead lights, the gleam reflected by the mirrors. Her toffee-brown eyes swirled with frustration.

She looked beautiful.

He swallowed past the lump in his throat. "Tell me something."

"Mercury is the closest planet to the sun."

"Something I didn't already know."

"I like your mustache."

His eyebrows shot up. "What?"

"Oh, did you know that already?" she asked, taking a seat next to him.

"My mustache?"

"Yeah, this hair above your lip." She reached up and traced it with her finger. "I remember when you started growing this. I wanted to touch it then."

His entire face warmed, in spite of the very cold room. "Wasn't much there to touch. Just peach fuzz."

"But you were proud of it anyway."

"You noticed it before anyone else."

"Not possible. It took me three days to get up the nerve to mention it. Your buddies must have said something before then."

"Nope."

"I don't believe you."

"You've always been very observant."

"Well, after I 'observed' your badge of masculinity and

'mistook' it for chocolate milk, did I wound your fragile ego?"

"Are you kidding?" He stared. She really had no idea the effect she'd had on him. "I marked the day on my calendar."

"Why?"

"A hot young babe saw my mustache, recognized it and commented on it. For a teenage boy it was an historic occasion."

Her eyes widened. "Me? Hot?"

"Did you ever look in a mirror back *then*?"

"Not if I could help it. I was too tall, too smart and too outspoken. I didn't need too plain to go along with it."

"I don't understand how you can say that. You were the prettiest girl in school."

"Now I'm sure you've been taken over by aliens. Quick. What's the square root of four?"

"Two, and if you're going to quiz me, at least ask a challenging question."

"Okay." She cocked her head. "Did you have a crush on me?"

"Ouch!" He grabbed his side as if wounded. "Direct hit!"

Her eyes went wide. "I never guessed."

"Duh! I hung around you all the time. Memorized your locker number and combination."

"Too subtle. Besides, I thought you hung around to bug me, to prove you knew more than me. You always dribbled that public television science talk just like at the café the other day." She clamped a hand to her forehead and fell back on the wood dance floor. "No wonder I married Roger. I'm an idiot."

"Nah, you just look at the world differently."

"How? Explain it to me, Einstein."

"My hormones kicked in late. I was still trying to figure out how to walk and chew gum at the same time."

"You never chewed gum."

"Exactly."

She laughed. "I don't believe this conversation. Is this why you brought me up here? To blind me, freeze me, and regale me with your adolescent discoveries?"

"I just figured them out." He grinned broadly. "Don't you think that's good news?"

"You're a nut."

"Pure cashew."

"*Gesundheit*."

He chuckled. "Oooh, that was worse than the other one."

"Sorry, couldn't resist."

He couldn't resist *her*. She was perfect.

"So," she prompted, "what's the good news?"

"Oh," he said, still mesmerized by her, "Chicago's looking good again."

"Yeah?"

"Oh, yeah," he said and leaned closer.

Her eyelids fluttered and her voice sounded breathy. "You could have told me that on the phone."

"But I couldn't do this on the phone." He brushed her lips once, twice, and drew her deep into his arms.

"Glen, this isn't helping anything."

"Shhh, I'm living out a teenage fantasy."

"Oh. Well. Don't let me stop you," she murmured and kissed him back.

He held her close and knew this is where he always wanted to be. With Christi.

"Mr. Stark?"

Glen jumped, pitching Christi onto the floor. "Joey?"

"I, um, I'm sorry to interrupt, but, um, gosh, can't you find a car to neck in?"

Glen reddened. "Mind your own business."

"Gosh, Mr. Stark, I'm sorry," Joey said quickly, his voice breaking. "I just wanted to tell you I'm going to lock up."

"Big bully." Christi punched Glen in the arm and scrambled to her feet. "Joey, wait! Joey, you did right. Mr. Stark just needs to work on his people skills."

"Gee, Mrs. Farley," the boy said, a grin replacing his earlier blush. "From what I saw, his, uh, skills are fine."

"Yes!" Glen said, pumping the air with his fist. "I'm vindicated."

"Will you let me handle this?" she asked. "I've been thrown up on in public. I have experience with embarrassment."

Joey groaned. "Yuk, really?"

"Hazard of being a mom, Joey. Look, I'd appreciate it if you didn't mention what you saw up here."

"Oh, I won't Mrs. Farley, I promise. Your mom took care of mine when she broke her leg. Nurse Lillian is the best."

"Thank you." Christi grinned. "And yes, she is."

After Joey left, Christi sank next to Glen and started laughing. "Nurse Lillian saves another life," she said, and rolled onto the floor laughing harder.

Glen fell back onto the wood slats and moaned. "Maybe the way to break up our parents is to act like the insane individuals we obviously are. Then they'd be scared to get married."

Christi stopped laughing. She stopped making any sound at all. He turned and poked her. "Hey, you alive over there?"

"I'm thinking."

"How? My mind's in a haze."

"That's because when I kiss someone, they stay kissed."

"Now who's arrogant?"

She turned onto her stomach and lay her cheek on her crossed arms. "Simple statement of fact. Battling with you taught me a long time ago to rely on my strengths."

"And kissing is one of them?"

"I don't have a lot of skills but yep, kissing's one of them." She grinned broadly. "You doubting my word?"

"No, but I am wondering what constitutes a test."

"Let Christi explain it to you." She patted his head as if he were a small child. "You take a guy and a girl, put their lips together—"

"That part, I understand. Very well, in fact."

"You do, huh? Is this a ploy to get kissed again?"

"Would it work?"

"No. That's another of my strengths. I'm decisive."

"About kissing?"

"About everything."

"Everything? Hmmmm. Just how and when did you determine you'd earned the 'Good Kisser Award'?"

"Ah, I see the wheels turning, Glen. You want to know how many tests I conducted. Roger asked the same thing."

"That twit? I'm surprised he had the brains to ask."

"Why didn't you like Roger?"

"Because he was an idiot. He let you go, didn't he?"

The moment the words left his mouth, Glen knew he'd opened the door to an emotional quagmire. He'd just admitted he thought Christi would make a good partner—a life partner.

"Sorry," he groaned. "I don't want to open old wounds."

"Can't open what isn't closed," she said, her voice muffled by her arms. "I left Roger two years ago."

"What?" Glen sat up. "I thought, I mean everyone in town said the divorce was final just recently."

"I lied."

"You *never* lie."

"I did about that. I gave him an ultimatum. Either he settle down and be a father to his children, or I'd take the boys and leave." Tears filled her eyes and spilled over onto her cheeks. "You know what he said?"

Glen froze. Christi never cried. Never. Through all the years they'd fought, she'd never shed a tear. Seeing it felt like a kick to the gut. He wanted to comfort her, but he didn't know how. A flaw his ex had expounded upon more than once.

"What?" He swallowed hard. "What did he say?"

"He said, 'I double dare you'." She gulped air as rivers streamed down her cheeks. "Can you believe a thirty-year-old man said something so childish? About his own sons?"

"What did you do?"

"What could I do? He called my bluff. Worse than that, he came home the next day and said we were moving again. That was the last straw. If he'd asked or even discussed it with me, I might have given in. But no, he ordered it. So I packed us up, took what I thought was fair from our bank account and left."

"And he didn't notice?"

"He always went ahead when we moved. You know, started the job, stayed in an apartment."

Glen nodded. "I know the drill."

"First weekend he came home, he found his stuff packed and a message on the answering machine for every day we'd been gone."

"Did he come after you?"

"No. Didn't even call."

"Jerk."

"According to him I'm the jerk. *I* slipped out in the night. *I* stole his children from him."

"Who filed for divorce?"

"I did. He didn't contest it."

"You took the boys and he didn't even sue for custody?"

"Why would he? He never wanted kids in the first place."

Glen slumped back onto the floor. He hated Roger. As a teenager he'd been jealous, and later, sad to hear Christi had married below herself. Now, for treating her so callously, but even more for ignoring Tony and Drew, Glen loathed the man.

"What did you do? Where did you go? How did you live?"

"Very simply. It took me a while to save some money, and build up the courage to call Mama, ask if I could come home."

"Christi, I'm sorry."

"Not your problem." She sat up suddenly. "I made a mistake. Now I'm trying to fix it."

"It's not that simple," he said gruffly, remembering his ex leaving him, and how much it hurt.

"Life is rarely simple, Glen."

He gazed at her with admiration. She'd had a rough time, rougher than he'd ever thought about having. No wonder she held her sons so tightly. "I'm going to find an apartment in Chicago," he said, suddenly making the decision.

She swiped at a stray tear. "Because of what I told you?"

"You convinced me just how different our goals are. I

think I should leave before this . . . attraction goes any further."

"I know it's a brush-off line, but I've always wanted us
to be friends, Glen. We both enjoyed learning so much."

"Friends? Maybe."

"Chalk up the rest to black holes, alien invasions, or
teenage fantasy?"

"All three." Heaviness settled on his chest, like he was
about to say good-bye to his best friend. "No hard feelings?"

"No hard feelings."

"Then this is good-bye."

"Yes. Good-bye Glen, and good luck." Then she walked
out.

Chapter Nine

Sunday evening, Christi opened her door to Sarge and Glen, and arched an eyebrow. "Come in," she said to both men. "Thought you were working tonight, Sarge."

Her mother hurried in from the den, glowing. "Irvin!"

"Lillian. Don't you look lovely." Sarge hugged her and knelt to receive both boys, who charged him from the hallway. "How are my buddies?"

Tony and Drew smiled broadly. "Great now that you're here. Mom said you had to work."

"Hope you don't mind us dropping in," he said, glancing up at Lillian. "The Pit was kind of slow, so I let Joey handle it."

"Of course not," her mother crooned. "What a lovely surprise."

Glen rolled his eyes, and nodded toward the kitchen. Christi hurried after him.

"I thought you were leaving," she said.

131

He crossed his arms and leaned against the counter. "Dad heard about our rendezvous. He's bribing me with it to stay."

She frowned, but inside she couldn't help smiling. She didn't want him to go. Not just yet, not after they'd decided to be friends. "But Joey promised not to say anything."

"Joey didn't squeal. I did."

"What?"

"Dad tricked me."

She arched an eyebrow. "How?"

"He asked me a direct question."

She slid back against the counter and shook her head. He smelled like autumn itself—crisp and cool. "Some spy you are."

"What could I do? I don't lie to Dad."

"Exactly what did you say?"

"Yes."

"That's all? What did he ask?"

"He asked, and I quote, 'Did you and Christi go up to the second floor and make out?' "

She laughed, then covered her mouth. "You're kidding."

"I swear as a former Eagle Scout. Not two minutes after I got home that night he took me aside and said, 'Tell me something.' "

"Oooh, not fair. He used our buzz phrase."

"He asked me about making out, just like he'd ask if I took out the trash."

"Thanks a lot."

"You know what I mean."

"How could he know?" Christi narrowed her eyes. "Joey called him."

"Nope. I thought of that, but Dad swears Joey had nothing to do with it."

"Then how?"

"Lipstick on my collar?"

"I don't wear any."

He smiled at her. "You don't need it. Your lips are luscious and red all on their own."

"Well, thank you. Thank you very much." Her ego given a much-needed boost, she smiled. "How long did Sarge confine you to quarters?"

"He muttered something about Thanksgiving."

"Mama wants us all to sit down together. Is that too much to ask?"

"I guess not. Now that we've sorted out our, um, friendship. Any ideas about Dad and Lillian?"

"None. You?"

The couple appeared. "Hey look at that, Lil, they're not arguing," Sarge said.

Lillian indicated they all sit. "Shall we discuss the menu for Thanksgiving dinner?"

Sarge shrugged. "No need. I've got it covered."

"But we're having dinner here, Irvin," she said sweetly.

"I can't cook in this kitchen," he argued. "It's arranged all wrong."

"For you maybe, but since I'm fixing dinner, it suits me fine."

Sarge stood. "Who said *you* were cooking?"

Yes! Lillian had a proprietary attitude about holiday meals, plus she used every dish in the kitchen. Sarge was military efficient, never wasting a movement. Oh, yes, this would work. Mama and Sarge would *never* sort this out.

"But Sarge," Christi said, forcing innocence into her voice, "it would be much easier to have it here. The boys could keep themselves amused a lot easier than at your house."

"Exactly right," Lillian said. "We're four and you're two. It's simpler for you to come here than us to go there."

"Lil, we're just over the back fence."

"But not to carry china and crystal dishes. I'd have to load up the car."

"We don't need china and crystal," he insisted. "Glen and I have plates at home."

Glen winked at Christi and quickly added, "We've used my grandmother's china for years. It's tradition."

"Well, it's tradition for Mama to make *her* mother's famous cornbread stuffing," Christi countered.

"Dad prefers oyster stuffing. Besides, this kitchen *is* laid out all wrong. At our house we can whip up a meal in no time."

Christi stood. "We? You and Sarge? I doubt it."

Lillian laid a hand on her arm. "Now Christi, maybe Irvin's right. I am a messy cook."

"That's not the point," she replied.

"It is if you're on clean-up duty," Glen insisted.

She narrowed her eyes. "What does *that* mean?"

"I'd rather cook a quick meal at our place and leave few dishes, than wait around forever and be left with a huge mess."

Sarge cleared his throat. "I think if we just sit down and discuss this, we'll—"

"Who put you in charge of logistics?" she asked Glen.

"Now, Christi, let's be sensible," Lillian said.

Glen frowned. "She doesn't know how."

"Me?" Christi stepped closer, her mind unconsciously calling up resentment from their high school days. "You don't know how to compromise. Everything has to be your way."

"My way?" Glen closed the gap between them. "This

isn't about my way, it's about two families discussing a meal."

She glared at him. "At our house."

"No. At *our* house. Dad runs a restaurant, he's the best qualified."

"Mama—" Christi turned, but they were alone. Sarge, Mama and the boys had retreated to the den. "Now, see what you've done."

"I wound up in the kitchen with you again," he snapped. "What's with you today?"

"Me?" She stared at him, and lowered her voice. "You promised to leave and take your manipulating father with you."

"We're back to that, huh? Lay all the blame on Dad and Lillian is totally innocent."

"Glad you finally see the light."

"What I see is—Hey!" Suddenly Glen's coat sailed through the air and smacked him in the side.

Sarge handed Christi hers, opened the front door and shoved them both out. "Cool off!"

"What in the—?" But Glen's protest fell on deaf ears, or rather the closed—and locked from the sound of it— door of Christi's house. The wind nipped his nose and frosted his ears, so he shrugged into his jacket. "Man!"

"What am I, seventeen?" Christi groused. "He didn't even let me put on my coat. I could catch my death out here."

Glen held her coat for her and chuckled lightly.

"Don't you dare laugh, Glen Stark. This is not funny!"

He couldn't help himself. Laughter erupted from within and burst out, shattering the stillness of the afternoon. She clamped her hands on her hips, but her shoulders shook and a few giggles escaped.

"It's all your fault," she said, between giggles.

"Is not."

"Is too."

"Not."

"Too."

Christi burst into laughter. "What a couple of brats we are! We deserved to be shoved into the cold."

"No argument from me. Let's take a walk into town," he suggested, eager to be on good terms again. "Maybe we'll mature on the way."

"Okay."

Good. For a moment there, he'd been worried. Their friendship was new and fragile, and though they'd meant to point out Irvin and Lillian's differences, they'd pinpointed their own.

On impulse he took her hand and tucked it under his arm. His pulse picked up and he scolded himself. *Friends, Glen. Just friends.* No more kisses, no more giving into the attraction.

What to talk about? They ought to discuss their parents, but he was reluctant to bring it up, because once that problem was solved, they'd have no reason to get together. And he liked getting together. So, he tried to think of something friends discussed—besides work.

Come on, Glen, you can do this.

"Why did your mother quit nursing?" he asked as they turned the corner and headed for the historic center.

"After she nursed Dad through his illness, she said she'd had enough of hospitals."

"So she retired?"

"Yeah." Christi crunched through some leaves. "She worked part time for a while, did some private duty work, but nothing full time. I worried about moving in with her.

I feared we'd mess up her routine, but she swears having us home gives her a lift. Guess Sarge does that for her now."

A horn honked and the car's occupants waved.

"Looks like we're drawing spectators again," Christi said as she waved back.

To his own surprise, Glen waved too. "That's hard for me to get used to. People honking because they're happy to see you."

"No kidding. When we lived in the east, honking meant get out of the way." She glanced up at him. "Your mother was originally from Miracle, wasn't she?"

"That's why we moved here. When Dad retired from the Army, Mom insisted she come home."

"I remember the day you started school. You challenged me on every minuscule detail of that day's lesson."

"A geek's way of getting to know someone."

"Why didn't you just say, 'Hi, I'm Glen, what's your name?' "

"Because I wasn't good at that."

"Being the new kid must have been tough. Until I married Roger, I'd never moved away from friends and the security of a familiar town. Now I know what it's like."

"Tony's had a hard time, hasn't he?"

Glen felt her muscles tighten through his coat sleeve. She didn't say anything for a long time and he feared he'd overstepped the bounds of friendship. "I'm sorry. Is that none of my business?"

"No, I appreciate your concern," she said, pulling her hand from his. "It's me."

He missed her touch immediately and gave himself another mental kick for crossing the line again. Soon, they reached the historic district, paused to gaze into shop windows, and walked across the street to The Pit. It looked fairly quiet with only a couple of customers.

Joey came to the door. "Problems, Mr. Stark?"

"No. We're just taking a walk."

Joey frowned. "Am I supposed to keep that quiet, too?"

Christi laughed, and Glen's heart lightened. "No," she said, "no more secrets."

"Thanks," the young man said, obviously relieved. "I'm never quite sure. You know?"

"I know exactly what you mean," Glen said and nodded.

They continued back to their neighborhood, but he slowed his steps as they neared Christi's house. He liked walking with her, being with her. She was fun, a good conversationalist and a good listener. "I'm sorry I mentioned Tony."

"Actually, I'd like to talk about him, get a man's opinion, but we'd better get back. The boys have homework and I need to fold some laundry."

"Another time?" Glen asked.

"Please. Before you leave?"

He followed her up the front steps to say good-bye, but when she frowned, he continued into her very quiet house. "Where is everyone?"

"I don't know. I at least expected a lecture from Mama on arguing in front of company." She removed her coat and picked up a piece of paper from the living room coffee table. "Oh, they've gone over to your house to compare kitchens. Looks like they're working on a compromise."

"The boys, too?" he asked, having already guessed by the lack of noise that Tony and Drew weren't in the house.

"Boys, too."

"In that case, you want to walk some more?"

She hesitated. "You know, this house is so rarely quiet,

I'd kind of like to enjoy it while it lasts. Do you mind if we just sit and talk? I'll make some coffee."

"Sure."

"We can plan our strategy about Mama and Sarge in private."

"Absolutely."

When she handed him the mug and her fingers grazed his, fog overtook his brain and he couldn't remember what they were plotting. To keep from looking like a complete fool, he took a seat on the floral couch and grasped at the subject always close to his heart. "How's work?"

"Good." She sat next to him, kicked off her shoes and tucked her sock feet under her. "But ah, just listen to that silence. Isn't it great?"

"Yeah. No phones, fax machines, pagers." He grinned. "Or immature employees arguing over the top of their cubicles."

"You supervise many people?"

"Too many. Not enough," he said, relaxing against the cushion. "Depends on the kind of day I'm having. At my last job, I was a line manager for about forty people."

"Forty?" She sipped her coffee. "Sounds awful. Is that why you're starting your own company? So you can hand pick your colleagues?"

"I have no problems with subordinates, but the corporate machine gives me a pain."

"Oh, you just dislike being told what to do," she teased, setting down her mug. "That's why you want to form your own company, so you can be the big boss."

"Okay, I admit it." He put down his coffee and leaned forward, resting his elbows on his thighs. "My last job, we moved fast. I had the privilege of working with bright people, on the edge of the industry, coming up with incredible ideas. Some ideas were good, some weren't, but we investigated them all, learned from the bad ones and kept going."

"Sounds perfect. What went wrong?"

"A lumbering, steeped-in-red-tape conglomerate bought us out. I got writer's cramp from filling out so many forms. When they canned SAVEONE, I threw in the towel."

"SAVEONE?"

"A software program that I believe will revolutionize the wireless communications industry. It's fast, handles a huge volume of data and is easy to use."

"You're going to use SAVEONE to build Stark Communications."

Glen smiled to himself. He should have known she'd understand. She had a brilliant mind and a way with people. Why hadn't he discussed his work with her before?

Because his ex-wife had never been interested, and he'd been fool enough to let that influence him.

"Those fools thought the bugs couldn't be fixed, that it would take too long to market it. Quite frankly, Neil and I working together could get it out in six months."

"Neil? What happened to Shana?"

He paused and arched an eyebrow. "We're supposed to be plotting our parents' breakup. You sure you want to hear this?"

"Geez Loueez, Glen. You said you talked about work with your friends. We're friends, remember?"

"Absolutely." He grinned. "Well, Neil Jackson and Shana Matthews are buddies from the industry. Neil and I worked together for about three years. He's in Atlanta now. Just got married."

She untucked her legs, turned toward him and ticked items off her fingers. "Office space, money, legal details. Wow, there's a lot involved, isn't there? How's it going?"

"Not well. To be honest, it's falling apart before my very eyes." He stood, anxious to finally get it off his chest, and began to pace. "First I had a prime location, lost it, found another less prime spot, but missed the deadline. Venture capital came and went. Neil withdrew his financial backing then put it back in. It's frustrating. Every time I get close, when my dream is within reach, something happens and it slips away."

"What about the realtor I mentioned?" she asked, her soft brown eyes dark with concern. "Didn't he help?"

"Yes, but my choices were limited to begin with."

"Starting a business takes a lot of work," she said gently. "Give it time."

"I'm running out of time. I'll lose my partners at the end of the year. Neil's contract is up December thirty-first."

"Shana?"

"Her company downsized her. She's out of a job December fifteenth."

"Before Christmas? That's cruel." Christi's eyes went wide. "She's a single parent. How's she supposed to provide for her child, or buy gifts?"

"The point is I have to get a break soon, or everything will fall apart."

"Glen, don't worry. You'll pull it off."

"I have to."

"You will."

"No, you don't understand," he said, taking a deep breath. Might as well spill everything. "I can't fail with this, Christi. I don't have anything else."

Chapter Ten

Christi heard the desperation in Glen's voice and her jaw dropped. All these years, she'd labeled him as unemotional, cold, but here he stood, passionate about his work, passionate about achieving his dream. How could she have been so wrong?

"You will succeed, Glen. I'm certain of it."

"That makes *one* of us."

"I don't believe what I'm hearing." She frowned. "Glen, you are one of the few people I know who's good at everything."

"Right. Every-*thing.*"

"What are you talking about?"

"I'm talking about people, Christi," he said, his voice pained and hoarse. "I'm not successful with people. Work is all I have."

"You're being too hard on yourself. Maybe you aren't the life of the party, but you're a good person."

"Well, I wasn't a good husband." He sat and closed his eyes, his voice no louder than a ragged whisper. "I provided the basics: food, clothing, shelter, but that's about it."

"What? Are you saying you didn't love your wife?"

"Not according to her." A muscle in his jaw twitched. "You know why I never had any kids? She didn't want to have any with me. She said a man without a heart would be a lousy father."

"And you believed her?" Outraged, Christi leapt to her feet. "Glen Stark, how could you? Oh, if she were here right now, I'd . . . I'd. . . ." Poetic justice swamped her brain. "Ooh! I'd introduce her to Roger. They're perfect for each other."

His snapped his head up and stared at her. "You think?"

"Two selfish, hurtful jerks? You bet. Maybe they'd cancel each other out."

"Or spend so much time making each other miserable," he said, sounding relieved, "they'd let the rest of us live happily ever after."

Christi couldn't believe it. She and Glen had more in common than love of learning and a competitive past. They'd made the same error, married people who never saw through their outer shell. Roger had never believed she preferred motherhood to making money. Obviously, Glen's ex-wife never realized he had a tender side.

"Forgive me?" he asked suddenly.

"Forgive you? For what?"

"For feeling sorry for myself. To quote a friend, 'I made a mistake and now I'm fixing it.' "

"Good for you."

"Thank you, Christi, for listening. You're a good friend."

Ah, but she wanted to be more, much more. Until this moment, she hadn't realized how much. Oooh. Scary.

"You're welcome," she said, needing to change the subject. "Baring my soul makes me hungry. You want something to eat?"

She started to get up, but he took her hand and pulled her close. "No, really, Christi, I mean it. Thanks."

"Glen," she breathed, staring into his silver-blue eyes, "we shouldn't do this."

"I know, but I can't help it."

He touched his mouth to hers. His mustache tickled, but she didn't pull away. Instead, she kissed him back and her fantasy world opened again. This time she envisioned herself in white, Glen in a black tuxedo and her sons smiling up at them. That's when she knew. She'd fallen in love with Glen.

Scary. And totally without a future.

"No," she said, pushing him away. "We can't do this."

"Why not?"

"Why not?" She swallowed hard and stared at him. "You know why not. We're friends."

"I know," he said, trailing his index finger down her jaw line, "but kissing you makes me happier than I've been in years."

"It does?"

"Absolutely."

"Yeah, me too." Her resistance melted and she kissed him again. She knew she was grasping at happiness and would come up with thin air, but she couldn't help herself. "You'd better go home before everyone gets back."

"Yeah, you're right."

She walked him to the door, gave him one more kiss and whispered, "Call me later."

"It's a date," he murmured and closed the door behind him.

Christi leaned against the wood and sighed deeply. "Oh, Christina Pierce Farley, what have you done?"

Glen stood on the porch and breathed in the cold air. The sun had set. Stars dotted the night sky and a harvest moon spread gold across the lawn. Man, he felt good, so good, he vaulted over the railing into the backyard. Whistling as he walked, he crossed her lawn, hopped the back fence and strolled up to his own back door.

"You two make up?" Irvin asked from the kitchen table.

"Yes. Sorry about arguing earlier. Are Lillian and the boys here? Christi read me your note."

"You gonna make trouble?"

"Me?" He shrugged innocently. "No way. Just thought I'd apologize to them, too."

"Lillian took the boys for ice cream a few minutes ago."

"Mmmmm, that sounds good," he said, peeking into the freezer. "We got any?"

"No, that's why Lil took Tony and Drew out." His father looked him straight in the eye. "But you don't like ice cream."

"Got teased a lot about that. Thought I'd give it a try."

"What? Are you feeling okay? Christi didn't smack you upside the head or anything?"

"Christi's not a violent person."

"Did you fall, get hit by a car?"

"No. Why?"

"Because you're being nice to me."

He patted his father on the shoulder. "Yeah, I thought I'd start that, too."

Irvin shook his head, obviously confused. "Since you're in such a good mood, we decided to have Thanksgiving at Lillian's."

"Fine."

"And we'll share the cooking."

"Fine." Glen closed the freezer and opened the refrigerator door. "I'm hungry. How 'bout I rustle up some dinner?"

"Rustle up?" His father stood and put a hand to Glen's forehead. "Are you running a fever?"

"Nope."

"I've got to go down to The Pit."

"Looked pretty slow when Christi and I walked by. Joey seemed to have everything under control."

"Thought you didn't like Joey."

"Nah, he's a good kid. You're a good judge of character."

"I am?"

"Yeah." Glen grabbed a couple of items in plastic containers. "Baked chicken okay?"

"You're going to cook? You hate the kitchen."

But Glen didn't hear. "What?"

"Nothing. I'm going to call Lillian and tell her you've lost your mind."

He shrugged. "Okay."

A few minutes later, the phone rang. Glen's good mood hadn't dissipated. In fact, the longer he thought about being with Christi, the better he felt.

"Hey, Galloping Gourmet," Irvin said, "it's for you."

"Okay. Dinner's ready." He wiped a glob of homemade salad dressing from his fingers and picked up the receiver on the wall phone. "Stark here."

"Jackson here," Neil said. "What are you so happy about?"

Glen grinned. "Life."

"Ah, you won the lottery and we don't have to worry about venture capital after all."

"Why, is Dewey pulling out again?"

"Possibility. Thought I'd warn you, and ask a favor."

"Shoot."

"Mail me the latest budget revisions. I moved into a new apartment and I can't find anything."

"I'll do that first thing in the morning."

"Thanks. Everything else okay?"

Glen glanced out the patio door across the yard to the light in Christi's kitchen window. "Everything's great."

"Good. Let you know when I get solid info on Dewey."

"Good enough."

His father marched into the into the kitchen and halted. "Is that homemade dressing?"

"Of course. You think I'd buy it at the store?"

"When did you learn to make it?"

"Dad, I worked at The Pit for years. I'd be an idiot not to know how."

Irvin dipped a finger into it. "Too much onion."

"Sorry."

"You're not going to argue?"

"You're the expert." Glen had no idea why his father kept looking at him strangely. "Why would I challenge your recipe?"

Irvin shook his head. "I don't know. What could have come over me?"

They talked while they ate, reminiscing about the past, trading war stories about work. "I could use you in Chicago, Dad," Glen said once they'd finished their meal.

"You catering a party?"

"Not for food, for advice."

"You never asked my advice before." The older man

leaned back in his chair and raised an eyebrow. "Why now?"

"You've run a business for eons. I'm just starting out."

"I see." He shook his head, and added, "I'm glad to tell you anything you want to know."

"Thanks." Glen stood and held out his hand. "And I want to wish you and Lillian all the best, Dad."

"Yeah?"

"Yeah. I was wrong to interfere. I hope you'll be happy."

Irvin rose, took Glen's hand and pulled him into an embrace. "Thanks, son. You don't know what that means to me."

"I didn't before," Glen admitted, thinking about Christi and how good she made him feel. "But I do now."

Glen slept better that night than he had in years, and in the morning, still in a good mood, he showered, dressed, ate a huge breakfast and strolled into town to the post office.

The clerk recognized him from before and narrowed her eyes. "We can't guarantee overnight service."

"I remember." He smiled. "Two days is fine. Sorry if I was rude before."

"Oh, that's okay. Have a good day."

"I already am."

He walked outside to a perfect fall day. Sunshine lit a bright blue sky; gold, red and green dotted the trees lining Main Street and crisp, cool air filled his lungs. Ideal weather for a stroll. As he headed to The Pit, he waved to the teller at Miracle Bank's drive-up window, complimented Miracle Florist on their window display of chrysanthemums and helped his neighbor put groceries in her car. When he turned onto Route 66 and spotted Miracle

Tour's awning, he pulled out his cell phone and called Christi.

"Hey," she said.

He leaned against the brick façade at the corner and said huskily, "Hey, yourself. Tell me something."

"Chicago's O'Hare airport is one of the busiest in the world."

"I knew that."

"They have flights to Tulsa several times a day."

He grinned. "You inviting yourself for a visit?"

She lowered her voice to a bare whisper. "Simply reminding you home's a short flight away."

"I won't forget. Can I see you tonight, alone?"

"Cub Scouts, homework, you name it. Sorry."

"I miss you."

"Me, you too. Call me later."

"Absolutely." He hung up, took another long look at his hometown, and wished he could stick around longer. Christmas would be coming soon and he'd love to spend the holidays snuggled in front of the fire, watching the boys rip open their gifts.

Wait. Why couldn't he? His pulse raced as possibilities flooded his mind. He didn't have to move far away. With modern technology, he could set up shop within commuting distance. Yes! Why hadn't he thought of it before? Any number of nearby cities would fit the bill.

Like Dallas.

Yeah, that would work. Dallas was only few hours by car, and possessed a large telecommunications industry. Why not set up Stark Communications there?

No, wait. What about Tulsa?

Yes! Not only could Tulsa work, it could be *perfect*. Less than an hour's drive from Miracle, he could see Christi and the boys on a moment's notice. *And* he could recruit software developers from local universities and spend less in overhead.

Smiling, he hurried to The Pit, eager to get started on his future, which could be just a phone call away.

From that moment, Glen seemed to lead a charmed life. Thanksgiving went off without a hitch. All his calls researching Tulsa as a viable option for Stark Communications garnered positive feedback, and he saw Christi every day. Life was good.

Only one detail was left, to confer with Neil who was on his honeymoon. Glen was certain his friend would go for the idea, but until that happened and Stark Communications had roots, he kept the Tulsa plan to himself. No point in getting Christi's—and his—hopes up if the idea went south.

Still, he was happier than he'd ever been and the days flew by. Before he knew it, fall had faded into winter, bringing brisk wind, plummeting temperatures and two mid-December storms. Though the sun tried to melt it, Jack Frost held onto its light layer of snow, giving Miracle a Christmas card look and feel.

The residents took it to heart and covered everything with red and green. City Hall sported an illuminated angel on the roof. All the fire engines wore wreaths on their grills, and each restaurant, shop and office on Route 66 hung ornaments and candy canes, transforming the highway into a huge Christmas tree.

Glen strolled through the historic center on a regular basis and often stopped in at Miracle Tours. Today he peeked in and Christi beckoned to him, but he shook his head and pointed to the gold banner strung above the street. "Only ten more shopping days until Christmas."

She pointed at the calendar and rolled her eyes.

He shrugged as if to say, "Hey, I'm a guy. What do you expect?"

She rolled her eyes again and he winked. Why worry when he only had a few gifts to buy? One stop at the Old Factory Warehouse, a string of turn-of-the-century brick buildings that had been converted into an indoor mall and he'd be finished. Heck, he'd have probably even have the presents wrapped before the boys got home from school.

Unfortunately, fate had other ideas and after an hours-long failed shopping attempt, he called Christi, desperate for advice.

"For goodness sakes," she scolded, "why do men always wait until the last minute?"

"Hey, I tried, but they didn't have a million toys when we were growing up."

"The sheer numbers *can* overwhelm the unskilled."

"Unskilled? I prefer novice, thank you very much," he said, feigning indication. "I never saw so many action fig-ures, cars and trucks in my life. And video games?" He shuddered, remembering the racks and racks of systems, games and controllers. "I don't even want to talk about that."

"Would you like a few pointers?"

"Please?"

"Well...."

"Christi. Don't make me beg."

"Oh, don't sound so pathetic," she teased. "Drew would be happy with anything he could take apart."

"How about The Pit's van?" he suggested lightly. "It's been running rough lately."

She laughed. "That might be overdoing it."

"No way. That boy's a born engineer. But what about Tony?"

"I don't know," she said slowly. "Usually he has a list a mile long, but this year he said he only wants one thing, and he already told Santa."

"Oh, boy," Glen said, running a hand through his hair. "I guess we'll all have to go shopping together."

Christi roared with laughter, nearly blowing out his hearing. "Hey! Is that supposed to be a *subtle* hint?"

"Sorry. I know you and my sons are pals, but I guarantee your friendship can't withstand holiday shopping in a crowded mall. You're tough, Glen Stark, but not that tough."

He rose from his office chair, switched off the light and opened the drapes. A quarter moon half hid behind some clouds, so the room fell into near darkness. Peering across his backyard, he envisioned the day when they could all be together, and not in different houses.

"Glen? You still there?"

"Hmmm?" He forgot what they'd been talking about. "Oh," he hedged, "I'm trying to formulate a response that won't sound egotistical."

"Hah," she teased. "Not possible."

"Come on, Christi," he said, wanting to be serious, to talk about being a family. "Give me a break."

"Like you gave our sixth-grade teacher a break?"

Images of their elementary school classroom flooded his mind and he groaned. He could be in trouble now. One thing about Christi, she never forgot anything. "Now, be fair," he pleaded. "Isn't there a statute of limitations on my past?"

"Are you kidding?" she said, giggling. "For the first time

in decades I have the advantage over you. I'm going to use it."

Yep, he was in trouble. The incident appeared in his mind as clearly as if it happened yesterday. Their teacher made a statement. He disputed it. She argued. He strode to the encyclopedia, flipped the huge volume to the exact page and proved himself right. After that, no one challenged him, especially the teacher.

"Okay," he admitted, "I may have been a tad over-zealous."

She snorted. "A tad? Oh, please."

"Okay. Okay. I was an arrogant, conceited, pompous . . . stop me when you disagree."

"Keep going."

"Okay, you got me. Satisfied?"

"Hmmm, maybe," she said, her voice lilting and fresh.

"Only maybe?" he said, a persuasive argument popping into his head. "Well, maybe this will help you decide. Bring it on, Christi. Come shopping with me tomorrow and you can challenge me all you want. If you dare."

"Oooh, now you've done it."

"I hope so," he said huskily. "Please, Christi. Please come spend the day with me."

"Oh, well, since you said please," she whispered, her voice deep and throaty, "I guess I will."

"Good. See you tomorrow."

"Tomorrow. Good night, Glen. Sweet dreams."

"Yeah, you, too."

Glen hung up the phone and spent the rest of the night dreaming about her. Now if he could just find a way to make those dreams come true.

Chapter Eleven

Glen woke up eager to get started and headed for the kitchen, whistling.

His father sat at the table sipping coffee. "You're awfully chipper. What's going on?"

"Christi and I are going shopping. Need anything?"

"What are the boys going to do?"

"Stay with Lillian, I guess."

"Send them over here, all of them. I'll get the ornaments out of the attic and we can decorate the tree."

"You haven't bought one yet."

"I'll let Tony and Drew pick it out. Tell them to bring a couple of videos along in case they get bored with us old folks."

"They love being with you two and you know it."

Irvin grinned. "Yes, I do. You be home for supper?"

"Depends on how much I accomplish. I'll call and let you know. I'll have my cell phone and my pager."

"Got it. Now get a move on, it's not nice to keep a woman waiting." He indicated the back door. "Take the shortcut."

"Yes, sir!"

Glen saluted, quickly crossed his lawn and hopped the fence. Christi opened her kitchen door and he drew her into his arms for a kiss. She smelled clean and fresh, her lips tasted like mint toothpaste and her soft Christmas sweatshirt crushed like velvet against his body.

"If brass players are the best kissers, and trombone players are the best of the brass," she said breathlessly, "I think you deserve a medal for first place."

"I'm just getting warmed up. I intend to kiss you as often as you come within range."

She laughed and stepped back from him. "Oh, really?"

"Absolutely."

"Well, we'll see about that," she teased, her eyes sparkling.

Glen delighted in looking at her, and did so for a long moment before a noise in the next room brought him back to reality. "Oh, Dad invited the boys and Lillian to help buy and decorate a tree."

"Boys," Christi called, "did you—?"

"We heard," Tony said and both boys instantly appeared in the hallway, grinning ear to ear. "Can we pick out the tree? A big, tall, fat one?"

"Yeah, yeah!" Drew jumped up and down. "Come on, Grandma, you already combed your hair."

"All right, all right." Lillian appeared next to Tony and Drew, dressed in a hunter green pantsuit. "Do I look okay?"

"You'll blend in with the tree, Mama," Christi said. "Be careful Drew doesn't hang lights on you."

"I think she'd look pretty with lights," Drew insisted.

They all laughed and scrambled out the back door.

Suddenly Glen and Christi were totally alone. Quiet enveloped them like a winter coat and he forgot all about shopping. "Tell me something," he said huskily.

"Sure," she said, raising her lips to his. "Who was the first woman doctor in America?"

He leaned in, and blinked. "What?"

"I promised I'd get you," she said, her lips curving into a sneaky smile. "I've devised a little quiz—"

"Quiz?"

"To keep the old brain cells going."

"My brain cells are fine." He straightened and crossed his arms. "What's the deal? What are the stakes?"

"I ask. You answer. For every question you get wrong—"

"I'm rarely wrong."

She wagged a finger. "That ego will be your undoing."

No, the sparkle in her eyes, the lilting tones of her voice would be his undoing. Already, his brain began to fog. He could be in serious trouble. "Just for the record books," he said, stalling for time to clear his head, "what happens if I'm wrong?"

"I get points."

"And I get a kiss."

"What? You want a reward for being wrong?"

"Why worry? Percentages *are* in my favor."

"You're unbelievable."

"So I've been told," he said and winked.

She rolled her eyes. "For every question you answer correctly, you get ten points. Each question you miss, I get *twenty* points."

"That's not fair."

"It's incentive," she said. "A challenge."

"What do I win?"

She smiled coyly. "If you win, you get to choose."

"Okay, but I still want a kiss for every question I miss."

"Consolation prize? I'd better prepare then," she said, reached into a huge canvas bag and drew out some lip balm.

Glen frowned and held up his hand. "Wait a minute. Since when do you carry luggage? Hey, the questions can only come out of your head. Not fair carrying around an almanac."

"Rats," Christi said and removed the fat volume from her oversized purse. "But how will I prove you're wrong?"

Whoever said shopping was a chore had never hung out with Christi. Glen looked forward to this trip with great anticipation of matching wits—and lips. "Any disputes," he said, confident he was in a win/win situation, "will be settled over dinner using the reference book of your choice."

"Done."

Christi held out her hand. He kissed it and brought it up around his neck. "Now for my first consolation prize," he said, giving her a loud smack on the lips, "I haven't the faintest idea who the first woman doctor was."

"Elizabeth Blackwell," she said and eyed him suspiciously. "Why do I get the feeling I've just been flimflammed?"

Glen laughed and pulled her to the door. "Let's get going. The sooner I win, the sooner I collect my winnings."

The Old Factory Warehouse teemed with people. Winter sunshine streamed through the third-story skylights and glinted off oversized ornaments, splashing a kaleidoscope of colors over the shoppers. The scent of Douglas fir permeated the air and muted cries of joy and frustration echoed off the brick walls.

"It's beautiful," Christi whispered. "I can't believe this used to store drill bits and pipe."

"Mmmmm," Glen agreed, slipping an arm around her waist.

Christi longed to melt against him, to forget everything and relax, but they were on a mission and only had a few hours. "Stop stalling," she teased. "Time for your next question."

"Glen! Christi!"

He chuckled as Eleanor approached. "Saved by the 'belle'."

"Only temporarily," Christi assured him and turned to Eleanor. "Hi! I thought you were working on the books today."

"The agency is like a tomb. By now everybody's planned their holiday trip." She paused and eyed Glen's arm around Christi's waist. "You two getting anything accomplished?"

"Some," Christi said and tried to disengage from Glen, but he tightened his hold. "Thanks for giving me the morning off."

He winked. "Yeah, thanks, Eleanor."

Eleanor arched a golden eyebrow. "For a man in a crowded shopping mall you seem awfully happy."

"Very."

"Uh-huh." Eleanor started to leave but stopped. "Wait a minute. Where are your sons?"

"They're decorating the tree with Mama and Sarge."

"Oh, you two are *alone*. Hmmmm, go for it."

"I intend to," Glen said.

Christi flushed to the roots of her hair.

"Good for you, for both of you," Eleanor said and left.

Christi whirled to face Glen. "Why did you say that? In minutes all of Miracle will know about us."

"Good. Cuts down on the explanations later." He took her hand and pulled her toward another store. Christi halted at a jeweler's display window.

"It's beautiful," she breathed, placing a hand on the glass. A garnet ring sparkled against green velvet. Diamonds and gold surrounded her birthstone, emphasizing the gem's depth and fire. She'd wanted a ring like that since her sixteenth birthday.

Glen hugged her from behind. "Mmmmm, nice."

" 'In my dreams' nice," she said, glancing at the price tag. "Okay, let's keep moving," she said. "Next question."

He groaned.

"You're not doing too badly so stop complaining."

"What did you do, study all night?"

"Of course."

He'd missed four questions—easy ones. She suspected he'd intentionally guessed wrong just to lock lips, but she didn't mind. One more wrong answer and she'd win, but it couldn't be an easy one. What she needed was an intricate question that she knew and he didn't.

Why didn't I sneak that almanac back into my purse?

Inspiration struck her and they continued walking. "Name genus and species for the common fruit fly—"

"Too easy," Glen interrupted.

"—then spell both."

"Hey, not fair!" he protested, dropping her hand. "You know I can barely spell my own name."

"Yes I do. Aren't you glad you have an easy name to spell?"

"You're impossible."

She grinned. "Yeah."

He took her hand again and laced his fingers through hers, his touch warming her. "What's that old saying? The difficult takes time, the impossible a little longer?"

"Hmmm," she murmured, trying not to dwell on his meaning. "You bragging, or stalling?"

"Both."

"You're hovering on the edge of failure, buddy," she said, straining to keep her mind on the game. "You get this one wrong and I win."

They walked further and turned the corner into a short hallway. Instead of answering, he wrapped her in his arms and kissed her—thoroughly and divinely.

"Oh, boy," she rasped after breaking the kiss, "I guess that means you don't know the answer."

"I concede the spelling of *Drosophila melanogaster.*"

Just as his breath warmed her ear, his voice warmed her soul. For the first time in years she felt happy, truly happy, and she let out a long, deep sigh.

"What are you thinking?" he whispered.

"Oh, nothing, it's . . . nothing."

"Come on. Tell me."

"I can't. You'll think it's silly."

"No I won't. Please? Tell me something."

Christi lowered her eyes, half embarrassed by her school-girl notions and half empowered by them. "Well, I have this vision of you, you know, rescuing me."

"Really?" he said, delight in his voice. "I didn't know you were the fair maiden in the tower kind of woman."

"I know it's strange, but that's how I see you, as a brave knight of the realm."

"A knight, huh? I like it. But do I have to wear armor?" He grinned and shuddered in mock horror. "I mean, iron underwear? And what about rust?"

"Oh, Glen," Christi said, laughing so hard, she nearly choked on her words, "you make me feel good."

"That works both ways, Lady Christina," he murmured and pulled her farther into the hallway. "With your permission I shall continue."

He kissed her, a long, deep, slow kiss that thrilled Christi to her toes, and created a new fantasy image. Not the knight and the lady fair. Not the family happily living in Small Town, USA, but the best vision of all. A man and a woman bound together, heart and soul, for the rest of time.

No doubt about it, she loved Glen. Not like she'd loved Roger, but without fears or doubts.

"Perfect," she murmured. "Absolutely perfect."

"I can't argue with the truth, milady," he rasped. "Thou art perfection indeed."

"Oh, Glen, I—"

"We need to talk," he interjected, his voice serious and deep. "But not here. Let's forget shopping and go home."

"Yes. Let's."

They hurried home, but just as she closed her eyes to receive another kiss, something buzzed.

Her eyes flew open. "What was that?"

"Pager," he murmured, his eyes still closed. "Ignore it."

"Your pager?" Guilt stabbed her and she jumped back. "Oh, no, something's wrong with the boys. Call. Quickly. Please."

"I'm sure it's nothing," he said, drawing his pager from his belt loop. "Besides, your mom's a nurse."

"Exactly. Which means if she can't handle it, it's serious. Oh, forget calling, I'm going over there."

"Wait," he said, peering at the readout and blowing out a breath. "It's from Neil. He's been out of town."

"Thank goodness!" Guilt weighed on her shoulders like

a two-ton truck and she sank onto a kitchen chair. For the first time in years, she'd put herself before her children and had the scare of her life. "I'd better go get them anyway."

"No, it's early yet. Besides, they're fine."

"I know." The temptation to stay nearly overwhelmed her, but she couldn't. Her true feelings might come spilling out and she'd lose him. She'd lost Roger by giving too much, too soon. Losing Glen would devastate her.

"But?"

"But I can't impose on Mama and Sarge. I'm sorry."

"I understand." He nodded and gave her a quick hug. "I'll come, too."

"Okay." She gathered her things and started toward the door. His pager buzzed again. "Thought you fixed that."

"I did. Neil must have urgent news. I'd better call him."

"I'll go get the boys."

"Wait, please," he said, holding out his hand. "This won't take long."

"Okay."

She took his hand and was immediately pulled against his side. His body felt warm and strong, so she didn't really pay attention to his conversation until he tensed.

"What do you mean, financial suicide?" he snapped. "Did you look at the figures? We'd be saving ten percent in overhead—No. I refuse to live or work in New York or California. I want to be closer to—Fine. We'll stick with the original plan and base in Chicago. Set up the trip and call with the details."

"Problems?" she asked.

Frowning, he tossed his cell phone on the table and stepped out of her embrace. "Difference of opinion."

"You mentioned New York and California. Does Neil

want you to headquarter Stark Communications on one of the coasts?"

"To get SAVEONE up and running, we need software developers with knowledge of the latest technology. New York and California are the largest pools of talent."

"They're so expensive. The overhead will eat you alive."

"Exactly. Which is why we settled on Chicago."

"When do you have to go?"

"Neil's set up a site inspection for Friday."

"Friday? But that's right before Christmas."

"Yes, but I have to go."

"I know," she said, sinking into the chair. "You'll lose Shana and Neil at the end of the year. Where did the time go? Just yesterday, I walked into the gym for the reunion."

He sat across from her, took both hands in his and looked deeply into her eyes. "I want to ask you something, and I want your honest reaction."

Her heart pounded so hard, she was certain the whole world could hear it. "Just ask."

"Do you think . . . that is, could you?" He took a deep breath, stood and began to pace. "This is hard. I swore I'd never do this again."

"Glen," she whispered, "tell me something."

He knelt in front of her and cupped her face in his hands. "Could you and the boys come to Chicago with me?"

"What?" she asked, a lump forming in her throat. "What are you asking?"

"I know you don't want to move again, but I want you with me. Come with me on the site inspection." His gaze held hers, his eyes searching, hopeful. "Let Tony and Drew look around, get a feel for the place. Consider it a first step, a trial—"

The lump in her throat thickened. "Marriage?"

"Yes," he said hoarsely. "Will you? Can you?"

"Oh, my," she breathed and clamped a hand to her chest. "Do you mean it? Do you really want us?"

"More than anything."

Tears streamed down her cheeks. Did she dare say yes? Could she uproot herself and her sons one more time? She wanted her vision, but could she have it outside Miracle, away from her safe haven? Did she have the courage to try?

He grabbed a napkin from the table and handed it to her. "Please don't cry, Christi. I love you. Please say yes."

Her voice broke and she barely whispered, "Yes."

"What about the boys, what will Tony and Drew say?"

"Come to dinner tonight and we'll ask them together."

He lost his balance and fell backwards. "Oh, I don't know."

"Scared?" she asked, smiling through her tears.

"Terrified. And more than a little concerned."

"Why?"

He ran a hand through his hair. "Well, milady, this gallant knight professed his undying love and you have yet to reply."

"What do you think 'Oh, Glen you make me feel good' means?"

"I'm a simple knight, milady, you must spell it out for me."

"And you're such a horrible speller."

"Stop teasing, Christi, please. I need to hear it."

"Of course." She curtsied deeply then wrapped her arms around his neck. "Glen Irvin Stark, knight of the realm, protector of the weak, loyal servant to the crown, I love you."

"Yes!" He whooped like a kid with a new toy and twirled

her around until the kitchen blurred into a massive kaleidoscope. "Could this day possibly get any better?"

"It's perfect," she assured him. "Absolutely perfect."

On Thursday, Glen's perfection short-circuited.

Christi stood in the middle of her living-room floor, looking cute and disheveled in a pair of red and green Christmas sweats. "Glen, Drew is sick. I can't take him on an airplane."

"I understand, but your mother is a nurse. She'll watch over the boys, and you can come with me. Please. Two days. All I'm asking is two days."

She paced from the couch where Lillian held Drew on her lap, to the kitchen and back again. "Don't do this, Glen. Don't make me choose between you and my children."

"I'm not. I'm asking you to leave the boys in your mother's capable hands for a mere forty-eight hours." Desperate to make her understand, he softened his voice. "I need you, Christi. I wouldn't feel right making a decision without your input."

"Roger always made me choose," she said, pacing again. "I won't do that anymore."

That stung. He wasn't like Roger, not in a million years. Her agitation must stem from a more complex problem than Drew having the sniffles. "Christi, why don't you tell me what's really bothering you? In private?"

Drew raised his head. "Go to Chicago with Glen, Mom. I'll be okay, really."

He lay on the couch moaning, while Lillian stroked his forehead. Tony stared and Christi paced. Glen felt as though he was the only one who didn't know the secret.

"I'm not going anywhere, Drew," she said. "You're right, Glen. How about the garage?"

"Not the kitchen?" he asked, trying to make her smile.

She glanced from him to where he'd practically proposed, and sorrow clouded her dark eyes. "No, not in the kitchen. Not ever again."

His heart hammered and he quickly followed her into the garage. "Christi, what bothers you, bothers me. Please tell me what's upset you."

"Don't make this harder than it is," she pleaded, her voice echoing off the concrete floor.

"Harder for whom? I don't want to go without you, but I have to leave tonight. I have a nine o'clock meeting in the morning. If I'm not there, I could lose my future."

He held his breath and watched her face. His Tulsa idea had bombed out because he hadn't considered the long-term effects. Graduates were in demand and moved up quickly. After a couple of years, his hot-shot developers would snag a better opportunity—in the big city, where opportunities and everything was more plentiful—and he'd be recruiting again. He didn't want to do that. He preferred to hire people for the long haul.

She sighed. "Then go."

"If I could postpone the trip, I would, but tomorrow is the last chance Shana, Neil and I have to look at this space."

"Then go," she said again.

What did he have to say to convince her? "I have a commitment to Shana and Neil. And," he added hoarsely, "I thought I had a commitment with you."

"You do. Or did. That is, until Drew became ill."

"Okay, I get it. You don't want to leave the boys. Fine, I'll go and be back in a couple of days. When Drew's better, we'll all go together."

"It's more than that, Glen," she said, backing away until

she leaned against the minivan, putting the hood of her mother's car between them. "Canceling this trip got me thinking. What if the business doesn't make it?"

"Is that why you look so worried? Security?" He relaxed slightly. "First of all, I'll make Stark Communications work. But even if it bombs, I'm positive I can find a good job."

"Where?" She stared down at her hands. "In Chicago?"

"Possibly, but that would depend on the opportunity—" Darkness suddenly swallowed him as if he'd fallen into a black hole. "This is about more than just moving, isn't it?"

"Much more," she said, hugging herself. "It's like a window to the future, Glen. I came to Miracle to put down roots, to provide my sons with the stable, loving childhood I had."

"But Tony's doing better in school, and I can still help him with it. Drew, too, if he needs it."

"When? Starting a business takes a lot of time and energy."

"I love those boys. I want to be a father to them."

"I know you do, but the moment Drew got sick I realized we've been living a fantasy, a dream. Anytime we needed you, you were there, day or night. Like a television sitcom dad."

He sucked air. "Or a gallant knight."

"Once you start Stark Communications, we'll never see you, and instead of Tony sitting by the door waiting for Roger, he'll be waiting for you." She backed away and lowered her eyes. "I can't put him or Drew through that again. I won't."

Glen's heart shattered. This was the very trap he'd worked to avoid—choosing between small-town security and success. "Christi, don't make me choose between you and my job."

"Then don't make me choose between you and my children."

"Why does it have to be either/or?" He racked his brain for a brilliant compromise, for a way to satisfy his needs and her wants. "Christi, please. Stark Communications isn't a job, it's my dream. It's *me*. Don't ask me to give it up."

"I'm not. I'm asking you to recognize the truth."

"What truth? Are you saying this is good-bye? Forever?"

"It has to be." Tears welled up in her eyes. "I'm sorry, Glen. I really thought it would work."

"I see." He swallowed, forcing words past the lump in his throat. "Perfection didn't last very long, did it?"

"It never does," she said hoarsely. "It never does."

Glen nodded, loathing Roger for hurting her, for instilling this fear of abandonment, and himself even more for not being able to come up with a workable solution. She couldn't leave. He couldn't stay. He couldn't be his father and give up his career for small-town security. Nor, like his ex-wife had demanded, could he sacrifice his future to prove he had a heart.

"Looks like we got sucked into a black hole after all."

"Looks like," she said, sniffling. "Good-bye, Glen."

"Good-bye."

Hurting so badly he could barely breathe, Glen trudged into the house, grabbed his briefcase and walked out of their lives.

Chapter Twelve

The instant the front door slammed, Christi sagged against the kitchen doorjamb, a horrible ache gripping her middle.

"Mom?"

Drew's plaintive voice twisted the pain and shoved it higher into her heart. "What is it, Sweetie?"

"Is Glen ever coming back?"

"Shut up, dweeb," Tony said, clenching his fists. "We don't need him. He left. Just like Dad."

Drew burst into tears, forcing Christi to ban all conversation relating to Glen, at least until she could discuss it without feeling so empty.

Except the hollow pain never went away.

By evening, Drew was feeling better and begged to play with the boy next door. Christi kept him in, so he sulked in his room. Dinner consisted of bowls of cereal, but none of them ate anything and depression settled over the house like a shroud.

Still the pain wouldn't go away.

Sleep didn't help, because she didn't get any, even after crying her eyes out. Instead, she lay awake, listening to the creaks and groans of the house and replaying Glen's exit over and over like a bad movie. He'd looked so angry, so . . . hurt when she'd compared him to Roger. Was she wrong? Had she condemned Glen without giving him a chance?

Uncertain of anything, she stumbled out of bed and into the kitchen, hoping to find clarity in a cup of coffee. She found dawn, with pale pink and orange rays slanting through the window—onto the exact spot where Glen had knelt and professed his love.

He'd looked so sincere, so real, and she'd been so hopeful. Had she been right to break it off, or had she destroyed a good chance at happiness? "Oh, Christina Marie Pierce Farley," she moaned aloud, "what have you done?"

"Mom?"

Christi whirled around to face the voice. "Tony? What are you doing up?"

"Thinking," he said, huddled in the corner of the couch.

She sat next to him and pulled him close. "About what?"

"About you," he said, his brown eyes so serious. "I'll never leave you, Mom. Not like Dad or Glen."

Oh, no, her little boy was trying to be a man again. "Thank you, Sweetie," she said gently, "but what happens when you grow up and fall in love?"

"I won't. Love hurts too much."

"No, Tony, don't give up," she said, stroking his hair. "Don't let Daddy and Glen keep you from loving. Love is what makes life worth living."

"I'll have love. I'll have you."

"Yes, you will, always. But I'm talking about the kind of love that a man and woman share, the kind of love that feeds your soul and makes you complete. The kind of love everyone needs to feel whole."

Oh my goodness!

The sun still hung low in the sky, but in Christi's mind it was summer in the desert. Bright, brilliant and so obvious.

"I am such a fool."

"What?" Tony gazed up at her as if she'd lost her mind.

Christi laughed. "I'm too sleepy to know what I'm saying, so don't try holding it against me."

He laughed, too. "Aliens take over your body again?"

"Yep. Zapped my brain, too."

How long had Roger forced her to ignore her own needs? She'd become so used to putting herself on the back burner, she wasn't even on the stove anymore. Heck, she'd shoved herself into the freezer.

Until Glen had thawed her out. He'd opened her up, understood her, connected with her mentally and emotionally. She'd felt alive and complete. Then, like an idiot, she'd pushed him away, afraid he'd add to the hurt Roger had dished out so often. She had to see him, to explain, to apologize. First she had to make sure the boys understood.

"Tell me something," she said gently.

"Sure."

"Why did we move here?"

"To put down roots."

"And what are roots?"

"Home."

"And what's home?"

"The place you live with your family."

"And who's our family?"

He rolled his eyes. "Mom, you're not making sense."

"Please, Tony, answer the question."

He grimaced and recited as if he were in school, "Family is the people we love, me, you, Drew, Grandma, Sarge. . . ." He paused and stared at her wide-eyed. "Oh, boy. You love Glen, don't you?"

"Oh boy is right. Yes, I do love him, but I messed up."

"You gotta call him. Apologize."

"Actually, Dude," she said, swallowing hard, "I thought I'd fly up there and talk to him in person. Grandma will be here with you."

"Then get going, Dudette." He stood and handed her the cordless phone. "Call the airlines."

"Someone going somewhere?" Drew asked from the doorway. "Is that why you're up so early?"

Christi held out her hand and pulled both boys into an embrace. "I'm going to Chicago to talk to Glen."

" 'Bout time," he said and went back to his room.

Tony shook his head. "He cuts right to it, doesn't he?"

"Yeah," Christi said, sighing. "Wish he'd told me that yesterday."

"You had to figure it out, Mom. Just like me and math. No one else could do it for you. Now, call the airlines and go talk to Glen, before he thinks you don't love him anymore."

"I'll give it my best shot." She took a deep breath, crossed her fingers and punched in Eleanor's number. To get a flight this close to Christmas she needed an expert.

"An expert couldn't have found better office space," Neil said. "Shana, you're a miracle worker."

"It is the right price, in the right part of town, and has

the right configuration for our purposes," Shana agreed. "But I can't take the credit for finding it. Glen gave me the realtor's name. I simply showed up to explain our needs."

"Well, it's like it was made for us," Neil said. "Don't you think so, Glen?"

Glen crossed his arms and gave the space a thorough once-over. Navy carpeting, pale blue walls, dark wood desks and computer ready. Neil was right. If Glen had commissioned an office to be built, he couldn't have done a better job.

Then why wasn't he jumping up and down excited?

"Glen?" Neil prompted.

"Yeah, it's perfect," he replied without enthusiasm.

He should be ecstatic, thrilled, adrenaline pumping beyond belief. This is what he'd dreamed of for years and now Stark Communications was whisper close to becoming a reality.

Yet, he wasn't ecstatic or thrilled or pumped with adrenaline. In fact, he couldn't breathe deeply and had trouble concentrating. The moment he'd landed at O'Hare the night before the pain had gripped him and steadily increased. He'd be concerned for his health, except he knew the cause.

Christi.

He missed her so much, he couldn't see straight. Every woman resembled her. Even Shana, a tall, autocratic blue-eyed blond reminded him of Christi.

Shana waved a hand in front of his face. "Glen? Is something wrong? Isn't this exactly what we need and want?"

Neil came at him from the other side. Glen didn't dare look up, fearing he'd see Christi's face on the African-American male.

"Yeah, Glen," Neil said. "If something's wrong let's keep looking. This is your brain child and you know best what will work. I can wait. I still have a year's worth of severance."

"I don't," Shana said firmly, "and I have a daughter to support."

"The place is fine," Glen muttered and moved to the window. Traffic snarled below him in the foot of snow blanketing Chicago. Funny, in Miracle the snow had looked magical. Here it just looked miserable.

"I hear you saying it, buddy," Neil said, "but I don't believe it."

"Yeah, Glen, what's bothering you?" Shana asked. A horn honked below and she joined him in gazing down at the cars jockeying for position. "Getting cold feet?"

"Just thinking about moving details," he lied. "Luckily, you won't have to deal with that. You already live here."

"Luck?" she said, glaring out the window. "I hate Chicago."

Glen stared at her. "But you've lived here all your life."

"That's right. I'm solid. Dependable. Not going anywhere. And what do I get for it? Laid off. Replaced by a college graduate, so the company can save a few lousy thousand for a couple of years."

"Neil said something just like that."

"When you were talking about Tulsa," Neil insisted.

Shana frowned. "Tulsa? What do you mean? Glen?"

"I had a crazy idea about basing us in Tulsa. The cost of living's cheaper, so is office space and labor."

"But that's not where you're from," she said.

"Miracle," he said as a wave of homesickness nearly knocked him off his feet. "Small town. Neighbors watch your house, even when you don't want them to."

Neil snorted. "How quaint."

"I've always wanted to live in a small town," Shana said wistfully. "Tell me, do kids play outside?"

"Of course. Tony and Drew practically live outside. They walk home—"

"Who are Tony and Drew?" Neil asked.

"They *walk* home?" Shana asked, arching both eyebrows.

Glen turned, drew a picture from his wallet and paused. The boys sat on Santa's lap, grinning ear-to-ear. He felt like he'd abandoned them. "Tony and Drew Farley," he explained past the lump in his throat. "They live behind me, uh, behind my dad, behind the house I grew up in."

"Alone?" Neil teased, "or is there a mom attached to these two?"

"They're adorable." Shana indicated the Christmas tree in the background. "Where was this taken?"

"Miracle's an old boom town. Route 66 runs right past several old warehouses and factories. The historical society restored two of them and turned it into a three-story mall."

"The mom?" Neil insisted.

"Christi," Glen said. "She and I went to school together."

"High school sweethearts?" Shana asked.

"High school competitors." They'd come closer to being more, much more, but—

"That used to be a warehouse?" Neil asked, pointing at the photo.

"Striking red brick building, built about nineteen ten," Glen said, nodding. "The town's working to revitalize the four square block center and has renovated several as antique shops, restaurants and office space. Leasing costs are low enough to—"

Zap! Like lightning, an idea flashed into Glen's mind. The room above The Pit! Solid floor. High ceilings. Perfect.

Suddenly his pain went away, his chest expanded with a deep breath, and his brain cleared. His father had never left Miracle, because he'd already achieved his success. In Miracle, with Glen's mother, Irvin had everything he'd ever wanted.

Glen could have it, too, with Christi and the boys.

"Leasing costs are low enough to what?" Neil asked. "To draw in businesses?"

"Absolutely."

"You're not thinking about—"

"I am," Glen said, "But I won't ask you two to make this kind of change. We'd have to rework the whole business plan—"

"Minor details," Shana interjected. "The point is to get Stark Communications up and running."

"Now wait a min—" Neil began, but Shana cut him off.

"What are the schools like? How convenient is it to the airport in Tulsa? What about housing prices?"

"The schools are good and have after-school care for kids of parents who work," Glen said, so excited about the idea, he could barely stand still. "Tulsa International is about an hour away and the housing is solid. Not big or fancy, but comfortable. Reasonable, too."

"Okay, I get it," Neil said, rubbing his chin. "Instead of snagging developers right out of college, we'd hire people like Shana."

"Exactly," Glen said. "Solid, dependable people, looking for a place to safely raise their kids."

Shana leaned forward, her eyes bright. "I have two friends who'd move to a place like that in a heartbeat, both of them computer analysts."

"Neil?" Glen focused on his friend's face. "You in?"

"Well . . . I'd like to look the place over once."

Shana snorted. "Oh come on, Neil. Glen grew up there and look how he turned out."

"Thank you," Glen said, "but Neil has a new wife who'd like to be consulted about moving to Oklahoma."

Neil nodded. "I'll do that right away."

"Good!" Glen shook with them on the tentative deal, grabbed his cell phone and punched in the number for airlines. "I'll go back tonight and get things started. If I hurry, I might—"

"Get back to Christi before she realizes you're gone?" Neil smirked. "Now, everything makes sense."

Glen blinked. "What do you mean?"

"In July you were gung-ho to get Stark Communications up and running in the big city. A couple of months later, you suddenly get an idea about setting up in Tulsa."

Shana smiled. "Then you show up gruff and rough like some old grizzly bear."

"Has to be a woman," Neil said.

Shana shrugged. "It's the only logical explanation."

"Then you won't mind if I leave," Glen said, coat and briefcase in hand—and halfway out the door.

"Just invite us to the wedding," Shana called after him.

"Will do!" *If I'm not too late.* Eager to find out, he rushed outside, whistled down a taxi and headed to catch the next available flight *home.*

Christi gripped the phone. "What do you mean, there's nothing available? Eleanor, I need to go see Glen."

"Think what you're asking. With Christmas coming up and snow in Chicago, you'd get there faster on a slow boat to China."

"Is first class gone, too?"

"You can't afford first class, and they won't give agent rates on this short notice."

Christi moaned and paced the living-room floor. She'd packed, squared everything away with Tony and Drew, but she couldn't get out of Miracle. If she missed the last flight today, she'd have to wait until tomorrow, the Saturday before Christmas. She didn't have a snowball's chance in . . . well, it didn't look good.

"How about if I go to the airport and try stand-by?"

"You could," Eleanor agreed, "but you're taking a chance on spending the night sleeping in a chair and still being disappointed. Why don't you just call him?"

"No, Eleanor, this has to be done in person, face to face."

"Wait, I have an idea. Hold on."

Christi paced the room some more, drummed her fingers on every available surface and mentally rechecked what she'd packed. It didn't help. Fidgeting just made her more anxious.

"Got it!" Eleanor said.

"You found a flight?"

"You have to get to the airport within the hour—"

"I'll take it!" Christi blew her a kiss and hung up the phone. "Drew, Tony, Mama, I need to go right now."

The three of them hugged her and wished her luck. She threw on her coat, grabbed her overnighter and opened the front door.

A man stood there.

"Glen!" She dropped her stuff and jumped into his arms. "I'm so glad you came back." She kissed him and yelled back into the house. "Mama. Tony. Drew. Glen's back. He came back." She grabbed his sleeve and pulled him inside.

"What's all this?" he said, indicating the suitcase.

"I was coming to see you."

His eyes widened. "You were?"

Her mother and sons rushed out again and hugged Glen, smothering him with "hello"s and "welcome home"s.

"Now, go away," Christi insisted, "Glen and I have to talk."

Heart pounding, she shrugged out of her coat and drew him into the kitchen, to their "spot." Afraid to read too much into his return and anxious to know the answer, she twisted her fingers and paced. "Why did you come back?"

"To show you this."

He held out a paper, folded in thirds, with the words Stark Communications showing across the top. "What is it?"

"It's only a rough draft, you understand. And I have to talk to Miracle Leasing."

"Miracle Leasing? But don't they handle those old factories like above. . . ." Her breath caught and she couldn't speak. Did she dare hope? "Are you telling me? Does this mean?"

"Open it all the way," he said softly. "Read it all."

With shaky hands, Christi slowly unfolded the page and read aloud, "Stark Communications. Miracle, Oklahoma." She clutched the paper to her heart. "But how? Can you?"

"Chicago just wasn't right. I missed you. I missed home."

"Home?" Had she heard him correctly? Was Glen admitting he felt comfortable in the very town he'd vowed to watch disappear in his rearview mirror? "You think of Miracle as home?"

"I think of wherever you are as home." He gently took the paper from her hands and laid it aside. "I'll still have to pour most of my time and money into the company, just like you said. And it means a lot of traveling to market the product."

"But you said you needed college developers. I mean graduate software, um . . . oh, I don't know what I'm saying."

"I hope you're saying that we can start again."

"Yeah? But how, Glen? How can you do this?"

"Simple, we decided to hire people like me."

"Like you?" She hesitated, still afraid to believe he'd base Stark Communications in Miracle. "You mean handsome, intelligent bachelors?"

"No, I mean people who want a safe, secure town to raise their children." He brought her palm to his lips and kissed it. "Christi, please take a chance on us. I promise I'll never abandon you or the boys for my job—or for anything."

"I know you won't."

A lump formed in her throat, but every last fear disappeared. Glen wasn't Roger, never could be, and she wasn't the same gullible girl. Besides, living meant taking risks, and more than anything she believed loving Glen was worth the risk. "Yes, I'll take a chance on us, Glen, if you still want me."

"Absolutely," he said, and drew her into his arms. "That is, if you'll marry me?"

"Oh, yes," she breathed. Tears streamed down her cheeks. "I'm sorry I pushed you away but I was afraid. I've been nothing but a mother for so long, I forgot how to be anything else." Brushing away the tears so she could gaze into his eyes, she whispered, "Tell me something."

"Anything," he said hoarsely.

"Are you settling because of me? I don't want you to give up, or even scale down your dreams."

"I'm not settling." He kissed her, slowly, thoroughly and divinely. "I came to my senses. All these years I thought my father gave up success for his family, but I was wrong."

She gulped. "You were?"

"Success isn't money, or titles, or fancy office buildings."

"It isn't?"

"No. It's being here with you and the boys. Making you happy is my success."

"Oh, Glen," she murmured and snuggled inside his coat, "you make me feel so good."

"And I intend to do so for the rest of my life."

On Christmas Eve, Christi stepped into the small chapel of the church where she'd been baptized. Candles flickered, poinsettias graced the altar, and Miracle residents filled the pews. Her heart pounded and she glanced first at Sarge, who would give her away, then at the man he'd give her away to.

Glen. He smiled at her, his gaze urging her to come to him, to come home.

Home. Yes. She'd finally come home.

The minister walked in, the organ music swelled and Christi and Sarge strolled down the holly-strewn aisle. Friends and family wished her well along the way and with each greeting she became more giddy, more excited about her future. Sarge must have felt her shudder, because he held her close, his arm solid and strong.

When they reached the altar and the minister asked, "Who gives this woman?" Sarge croaked out his reply, but when she kissed his cheek, his voice was strong and sure.

"Welcome to the family, Songbird," he said, and slipped away to join her mother, Tony and Drew in the front pew.

With joy in her heart, Christi turned to Glen and promised to love, honor and cherish. When he slipped the garnet and diamond ring on her finger, the one she'd coveted at the jewelers, she knew she'd found her soul mate, a man who knew and loved her for herself.

She gazed into his silvery-blue eyes and whispered so only he could hear, "Perfect."

The minister pronounced them husband and wife, and Glen kissed her. Everything faded into the background as his warm lips sealed their vows. She clung to him, and eventually heard several people clear their throats. He merely drew her closer and she let him. When he finally raised his head, cheers filled the small chapel.

"You're right, Christi," he said softly. "Together we are perfect."

"Absolutely perfect."

Christi walked back down the aisle on her husband's arm, happy, confident and grateful. Thanks to a hometown reunion, she and Glen had rediscovered each other, and made a home in each other's hearts. And thanks to the miracle of love, she knew they'd reside there forever.